D1634826

George Milne – Cat Detective

Acknowledgements

I would like to thank everyone who read my first novel and encouraged me to write a second. To those who read my first novel and tried to discourage me from writing a second; I apologise. I would also like to thank Sandy Murray, John Orr and Margaret Rustad for their assistance with proof reading and other helpful suggestions. As ever, a big thank you to my mother Margaret Murray and my children Sebastien, Camille and Elliot for their encouragement. Also a big thank you to Misha, Corran and Finn McCallum for their encouragement too. Finally a special thank you to Pauline MacGillivray.

By the same author;

Body and Soul

The Treasure Hunters

George Milne – Murder at the Butler's Convention

A Snow White Scenario

For my parents and for my children.

Chapter One

David Harvey had been on duty at Accident and Emergency for 10 hours now and he was shattered. He had completed 60 hours that week so far with another 20, if he was lucky, before he could have a full day off. During his first few weeks after graduating as a doctor, a succession of strange domestic accidents and mishaps in the day-times had given way to drink-related injuries in the evenings. It was a familiar pattern he had got used to quickly here. Today, though, something was different.

He had been trying to grab a quick break with a cup of coffee and a sandwich around half past five. That was often a quieter spell, as casualties seemed to have a break for evening meal before continuing to injure themselves later after they had been drinking. Halfway through his second sandwich he had been paged. He headed back to A&E. An ambulance had brought in a man of 25 or so who had been severely beaten with a baseball bat. One of the nurses briefed him mechanically on the injuries. In addition to the skull, nose and jaw fractures, there was serious concussion. That was only the young man's head. Below that a list of breakages, bleeding wounds and internal damage found even David struggling for all the proper medical terms. The nurse finished with the added attraction of a deliberately severed finger.

The nurse, Fiona Rawlinson, had worked in A&E for 28 years and could have dealt with the casualties in her sleep. Indeed, she had done that often enough on night shifts over the years, but she was a nurse and therefore needed the authority of a doctor for many of the procedures and medications required. David knew all of this and felt the pressure. He also appreciated the guiding hand which Fiona had provided during his stint in A&E when he was hazy on what to do or just so tired that his brain was struggling. They had their own designated areas and levels of authority but these had to blur for things to run smoothly and for patients to get the treatment they needed. It was a game they had to play. David reamed off the treatments required for this patient confidently, with good reason, still annoyed at the interruption to his meal.

David wouldn't have minded quite so much but this was his third such casualty in four hours. In each case nobody had been kind enough to send in the missing finger in a bag of frozen peas. Indeed the second case already had a missing finger and toe from sometime previous. If they recovered, which was a no better than 50/50 chance for two of them, they would have to live with fewer digits. If they didn't, then the coffin would be just that little bit lighter for the pall bearers.

The regular staff hated it when the local drug gang did its house-keeping during their shift.

'Recovered' was also a matter of degrees. None of tonight's clients would fully recover from the trauma inflicted on their bodies by today's visitors. A damaged retina here, impaired hearing there and a strong chance that they would all be slightly hard of thinking for the rest of their lives.

It was all part and parcel of a junior doctor's learning curve in A&E after qualifying. David wouldn't have minded too much. The first case gave him a tough challenge and war stories to share with his recently qualified colleagues, but three in a row started to get a bit samey.

Chapter Two

George Milne eventually got out of bed at 11 o'clock. He walked through to the bathroom and took a long and much needed pee. Then he went to the kitchen, filled the kettle and switched it on. He took a large mug from the basin in the sink and gave it a cursory rinse under the tap. He did the same with a spoon he fished from the bottom of the basin amongst the remnants of the previous night's curry and rice and then wiped both with the filthy dish towel which was draped over the handle of the cooker. A quick visit to the fridge procured a half full carton of UHT full-fat milk. George sniffed it cautiously to confirm that it wasn't half way to becoming yoghurt and poured a generous dollop into the bottom of the large mug. Using the spoon he added two spoonfuls of instant coffee to the milk, noting as he did so that some coffee had stuck to the still-damp metal. Ignoring the residue of coffee on the spoon he next picked up a semi-solid bag of sugar and carelessly shovelled two lots into the mug, each one containing some stale coffee solids from previous days. By that time the kettle had almost boiled so he poured some hot water from it into the mug and switched it off at the mains. He stirred it slowly one way, then the other, alternating several times as he did so till he was sure the sugar and coffee had all dissolved. The spoon was thrown back into the basin ready for the next time it was needed. George picked up two chocolate digestive biscuits from an opened packet beside his bread-bin and walked through to the lounge, starting to eat one of the biscuits as he went. There he took a first mouthful of coffee and breathed in slowly before finishing the first biscuit. All of this was done without washing his hands from the visit to the toilet. Another day had started.

George put on the television and it slowly came to life as if it too could have done with a strong cup of coffee. After a few seconds the BBC news channel appeared with a well-dressed woman describing in great detail how shit the weather was going to be where George lived. When she was finished she wished everyone a good day anyway and handed over to someone in the States explaining the latest technology being introduced at an annual trade fair for geeks and geek journalists. He was very excited by it all but George was not. He was rarely excited by anything these days. Not football, certainly not cricket or rugby, or the weather. Pretty women would occasionally raise his spirits till he would accurately judge his chances of ever getting anywhere with them. At that point his spirits would return to their normal, rather dormant state.

All in all though, George was quite happy with the way his life was now. He had known worse: far worse. He had been married for 15 years to Glenda Morrison. He had known her since school and she had never been a looker. When they had had to learn country dancing each year before the Christmas party, she would always be the third last to be chosen by boys in their class. In fairness, George was usually chosen second last during a ladies' choice. Perhaps someone was ill one day but they found themselves dancing the Canadian Barn Dance together one Tuesday and a strange, uneasy friendship had developed; a friendship which had continued after they left school. Glenda got a job on the production line at Franny's Bakery and George had become an administrator in the local authority, dealing mainly with the paperwork to be actioned when people wanted to exchange council houses for whatever reason.

Cakes and paperwork had blossomed but nothing approaching true love. They became regular partners whenever either needed one for a social occasion; a relatively loose relationship which had served them both well for some ten years. Eventually Glenda had watched enough of her contemporaries get married and, with good reason scared she would be left on the shelf, she had popped the question to George one night. It had actually taken the form of an ultimatum

11

and George had reluctantly agreed to wedlock. Thereafter, Glenda's life had continued largely as before whilst George's had descended from unpleasant to sheer purgatory.

Firstly, he had had to move out of his mother's house and into a council house with Glenda. He had not been allowed to take any of his own furniture and fittings from his bedroom, a room he had lived in all his life. A few of Glenda's precious things made it from her parents' house to their new abode. Everything else had to be bought new. George's views on style and colour were never sought by either Glenda or her mother as they fitted out the new home. His wallet, however, was regularly needed and he quickly found that his modest savings account first became a joint account and then quickly thereafter, became empty.

Sex had never formed a part of their pre-marriage arrangement and little changed in this respect after the big day. The wedding night had seen a brief attempt at seduction by George which was quickly followed by separate bedrooms in the hotel. During the first few years of the marriage George had attempted to have sex a total of nine times with Glenda and had only been successful twice, both of these occasions being after the bells on New Year's Nights when Glenda had been slightly tipsy. Those two years had started badly for George with his period of disgrace lasting almost till February each time.

Glenda continued to work hard at Franny's Bakery and continued to sample a lot of their produce, putting on approximately a stone per year for the first ten years of her marriage to George. He had watched her go from a size 14 to a size 22 in that time and slowly lost any desire to consummate their relationship further.

He realised that although he had not been deliriously happy before they married he was miserable afterwards. Any flexibility in terms of his leisure time had disappeared and with it most contact outwith the workplace and his wife's immediate family; in other words her mother. This even extended to his choice of television programme coming a poor third to the choices of Glenda and Mrs Morrison, even when his wife was out of the house.

The only exception to this was a Friday and a Sunday night when his wife and her mother went to the local Bingo Hall. On these evenings he would be left alone from about seven in the evening until they returned at around ten thirty. It was assumed at first by the two women in his life that he would stay at home on these occasions and tidy the dishes or watch his own choice of television. They had reckoned without a well hidden and fairly shallow rebellious streak inside

George which led him into the temptation of actually going out alone. It had taken him a few weeks to pluck up the courage and he was assisted by a colleague's farewell party being held in the nearest pub to George and Glenda's matrimonial home, The Ranch.

On this particular Friday, George had warned off Glenda sufficiently to gain her permission for him to attend The Ranch for an hour or two to bid a fond farewell to somebody called Jack, who was leaving one department in the local authority to take up a slightly better post in a different department. It would be stretching things to say that he attended this function with Glenda's blessing, but she had agreed to him going for no more than two hours as long as the dishes were washed and dried before he left and that he was not drunk when she and her mother returned from the bingo.

George had readily agreed and arrived home early from work to shower and change into what he laughingly referred to as his glad rags. It had been many years since anyone would have described them as glad, or happy or even suitable for a party of any kind. To George, however, they represented the freedom of his younger days, such as they had been. As he dressed he realised that he was wearing them to go out alone for the first time in over 15 years.

The night had been a rather dull affair, saying farewell to a rather dull colleague that no one would miss but to George it had given him a taste of freedom that he was not prepared to give up lightly.

As a result the following Friday he had again dressed in his glad rags, once his wife and mother-in-law had safely left and headed down to The Ranch for a game of darts. He had noticed a few of the locals playing darts during the previous week's visit and he had decided that if the ladies could play bingo twice a week, he would play darts.

As he arrived at the pub, the barmaid nodded hello to him and asked if he would like a pint of 70 shillings again. It was not a busy pub and the barmaid didn't have to remember many regulars but this very feat of recall made George feel a bit special and somehow, as if he belonged.

He plucked up the courage to ask if he could join in a game of darts and with a bit of friendly banter he was paired up with a regular called Callum. Callum could play a bit but tonight's game was just a bit of friendly practice, so he didn't mind when George hit the wall or the blackboard instead of the dartboard itself. Although George was a dreadful player the others were so used to each other's company that they were delighted to welcome fresh blood into their group.

George was very careful to return home early before Glenda and her mother, who often stayed over for the weekend in the spare room. She only lived a quarter mile away from the house and was perfectly capable of walking the distance with ease but Glenda wouldn't hear of it when it was dark outside, and George was never consulted. Glenda was worried her mother might be attacked on the way home. George was sure nobody would dare.

The furtive trips to The Ranch on a Friday continued and even stretched to an occasional visit on a Sunday night too, although the darts players didn't always play on Sundays. Instead George would find himself amongst a select group of individuals recovering from a heavy session on the Saturday night or extending the weekend as long as possible to avoid the thought of Monday morning.

George didn't mind the thought of Monday morning at all. After all it got him away from the house, from Glenda and was the day her mother went home. In fact, compared to the rest of the Sunday night customers at The Ranch he positively looked forward to it. Despite this he would join in the banter as everyone distracted themselves with talk of football, women and television programmes or films they had watched over the course of the weekend.

In time Glenda realised George was leading a double life but as he never appeared to be drunk and seemed to be in much better humour with his mother-in-law, she let it pass.

If sex is the corner stone of love and love is the corner stone of marriage there was actually very little structural support to keep George and Glenda together. They began to argue often, although George made a point of never joining in. Things came to a head one day when Glenda and her mother had a blazing row in the house in which Glenda and George cohabited. Glenda implored George to come to her aid and, as he had no real understanding of the cause or strong feelings regarding either side of the argument, he refused. Mrs Morrison had stormed out, slamming the door behind her, leaving George to face his wife's rage at his lack of support. Things went from bad to worse as he briefly stated his reasons and Glenda raged on and on that he had refused to support her against her mother in a very similar way to when she had raged over his lack of respect to her mother in the past. After a long and unpleasant half hour she had stormed off to her mother's house.

Despite previous arguments, George had a feeling that this one was a final stage and took the precaution the following day of changing the locks on the doors of the house to ensure that it was. He had then gone off to The Ranch for a rare delight, a pub lunch. Whilst he was there Glenda had returned to find the doors barred to her. She immediately arranged for a locksmith to force his way in and with the help of her now sympathetic mother removed all her things. When George returned that evening he realised that the locks had been changed back but through a combination of determination, alcohol and a now greatly weakened doorframe, he was able to cave in the backdoor and fall asleep on the kitchen floor.

The following weeks were a blur of telephone calls from both Glenda and Mrs Morrison threatening that if George didn't change his ways Glenda would not be returning to the marital home. George took considerable resolve from this and his ways did not change one little bit. Thereafter lawyers became involved at Glenda's tearful insistence and the phone calls from Mrs Morrison largely stopped, being replaced by one call George made each Friday to his own lawyer. After a few such calls George's lawyer suggested he would just phone George when things had been finalised and there were papers to sign. This arrangement suited George fine. To prevent any further direct contact with his ex and her mother he blocked their numbers on his phone and also that of Mrs Morrison's neighbour, a Miss Balfour, who had never liked George (or indeed any man) and had put her phone at their disposal.

The divorce ran its course and after just over six months, George was again a single man. He celebrated with another pub lunch although this time round he remained sober enough to open the door with his key.

Chapter Three

Detective Constable James "Jimmy " Bell had joined the police in Glasgow and had been transferred to Coatshill after ten years, on promotion to sergeant. By then he had already joined CID where he believed he belonged. He was happy enough with the change of scenery and could easily commute from his house in Lenzie on the outskirts of Glasgow. It was a bonus both to him and the local station that he was a stranger in the town and he had been sent out under cover at first to gather intelligence on all the troublemakers in town. Principally this meant getting as much information as possible on the supply of hard drugs in the area and the related crime it spawned. He had achieved a measure of success and, when he had become too well known in the locale to continue in this role, he had been seconded to a team trying to reduce the flow of drugs by putting as many offenders in prison as possible.

It was in this guise that he had been sent down to the local accident and emergency to see if any of the latest batch of gang victims were prepared to blab about who had attacked them. He wasn't hopeful and as usual his instincts were right. The duty doctor, a young but already world-weary lad called David Harvey, had filled him in on the night's clients.

"Three victims of assault with a baseball bat, or similar. Additional wounding from fists and boots. Also in each case the patients had had a finger or toe removed, probably with a pair of secateurs." Dr Harvey had paused to ensure DS Bell was paying attention, which he was. "Early indications are that all three will survive but it is likely to be a good few hours yet before any of them are in a fit state to talk, assuming they agree to talk to you."

"Sounds like Wacky Frank and his boys have been busy then," Jimmy Bell commented.

"Who?" inquired David Harvey.

"Off the record, they have been paid a visit by Francis Eric Cook Esq. and/ or some of his associates. He is better known as Wacky Frank because he started by selling wacky baccy to his school mates, although I gather he didn't have many mates even then. The finger or toe thing is his calling card. I suspect they owed him money and didn't pay on time. Looking at who you have down here, that seems likely. Either that or they tried to kick the habit and Frankie wasn't supportive. He is very much against his customers giving up drugs. It's bad for business."

"Are you going to hang around to see if any of them feel like talking about what happened?" Dr Harvey asked.

"I might as well," Jimmy replied, "although nobody is ever keen to spill the beans after Frankie's clipped one of their fingers off. I've nothing better to do and you never know, one of these days he might just make someone angry instead of frightened."

David Harvey headed back to his patients, the three from earlier who were still unconscious and a selection of others who were very drunk and had injured themselves as a result. The only other patient was an elderly lady who was neither drunk nor an obvious substance abuser. She had tripped over her Yorkshire terrier and fallen down some stairs. As a result, her hip was broken and she would be hospitalised for some time. Despite being in considerable pain, her only concern was for the dog. It had survived unscathed but there was nobody to look after it and the lady was desperately worried about it. Dr Harvey almost admitted to her that there was a policeman along the corridor who might be willing to help but decided on balance that Jimmy wouldn't have thanked him if he had. In fact, he wondered if Jimmy might have had the dog put down just to emphasise the point.

Chapter Four

George had left his mother's house reluctantly to move into a council house with Glenda when they got married. It had been the only house he had known and his room held all the treasures of a happy childhood. He was dissuaded from taking any of his personal possessions with him and as a result he had never felt fully at ease in the matrimonial home.

When his mother died two years after his divorce, George inherited her house and all that it contained, including the contents of his bedroom, largely untouched during his absence. The house was actually a two bedroom flat on the ground floor of a four-in-a-block building of similar properties; what local estate agents would refer to as a cottage flat. Mrs Milne had taken the opportunity to buy the flat through the government's right-to-buy scheme and had managed to pay off the mortgage some years before her death. George required no time to decide what to do with it or where to live after his mother's funeral was past. He moved back into his old room as if he was putting on a favourite coat, long thought lost.

His mother's room had been emptied of personal effects by her sister, who also took away anything of monetary value which she could find in the house. George didn't mind. Although he missed his mother greatly, he realised that her final years had been punctuated with suffering and, as the minister had said at her funeral, she was now at peace and free from all pain. Thus George moved back in, viewing the turn of events as something of a win/win for both his mother and himself and with a completely clear conscience. He had simply gone home as his mother no doubt had wished.

George had never really enjoyed his job at the local authority. He needed a job to earn a living, especially after he got married to Glenda but it had never been something he found exciting or challenging. It was more of a habit than a career. Admittedly he had looked forward to getting out of the house each day while married, but after the divorce he had started to feel bored and unsettled. It was too late to embark on most other careers but it was more a desire to leave his job that he felt rather than a specific desire to do something different.

Shortly after he had moved back into his mother's old house the Council in Coatshill decided to have one of their regular cost-cutting exercises focused round the reduction of staff levels by about 5% across the board. As ever, people with families and mortgages grew pale and started to worry for their future. George, however, started seriously considering what this might mean for him. Rather than a disaster as it would be for many of his colleagues, redundancy could be a means of escape for him. He had no mortgage on his house. He had built up a few thousand pounds again after the divorce which had been augmented by his mother's savings. If he took the redundancy package on offer, then after his many years of service he would be able to put away quite a tidy sum. His needs were very modest and he could make the money go a long way. If necessary he could get a part time job somewhere or even take in a lodger, in extreme circumstances. Either way he was sure he could manage to survive and the thought of not having to come into work each day and sit at his computer and phone, listening to the drivel and trivia of tenants' lives was too powerful to resist.

Having made the decision he put in an application for redundancy to a rather surprised HR department and waited. They acknowledged the application almost by return and in a few days he received written confirmation that they would consider his request in line with future staffing needs in his department and enclosing a breakdown of his entitlement if he was selected. The sum was greater than George had calculated, largely because he had forgotten to take any holidays that year as usual.

Then he had to wait while decisions were made. Rumours were rife in all the departments and the redundancies were the main topic of conversation for weeks. Ironically, while George had to wait hoping that he would be selected to go, he had to listen to the concerns and panic of colleagues who were terrified that they would be chosen instead. Somehow it didn't seem to be as hard a decision as HR made it out to be. George could have taken the decision for his department of 19 people in about two seconds flat.

Eventually decisions were finalised and signed off by the senior HR manager who had been on holiday for a fortnight while things were sorted out. Envelopes arrived for everyone and had to be signed for. George opened his straight away and was delighted to find out that he was to be paid off in two weeks' time. The Coatshill Council thanked him for his years of loyal service and wished him the very best in the future. The rest of his department were relieved to discover that their jobs were safe for now with the exception of Mary Johnston who, inexplicably, was also to be paid off against her wishes. She burst into floods of tears and being fairly young and attractive had to be comforted by everyone in the room.

George went home that day and marked the last day of work on his calendar and started ticking off each day as it finished. He celebrated the good news with a trip to The Ranch and after consuming considerably more than his customary intake of beer had to phone in sick for the first time in years the next morning as a king size hangover kicked in.

Two weeks later, on a Friday, a mass farewell do was organised by the council for those who wished to attend after work. It was held in one of the local hotels with Franny's Bakery, as ever, providing the buffet. As the food and the first few drinks were free, there was a large attendance, including some of the councillors themselves who never visited many of the departments but rarely missed a free meal. Mary Johnston was conspicuous by her absence but the rest of George's department had turned out in force to wish him farewell. There had been a collection, and as no one had a clue what George's hobbies were, he was handed an envelope with £100 in it from his team leader after a rather amusing speech. Unusually for George, he stayed till the very end and treated himself to a taxi home, paying for it with some of the money from his farewell gift.

The following day George had the worst hangover of his life, having mixed free wine with bought beer all night. Despite this he was in great spirits. Through a combination of being a single child and good luck he had managed to escape work whilst still under fifty, with a reasonable prospect of never having to work full-time again. Life was good.

Chapter Five

George didn't like cats and never had. He didn't actively hate them necessarily, but he certainly didn't actively like them either and wouldn't have had one in the house if his mother hadn't made him swear on her death bed to look after Pebbles as long as she lived. After his mother's death, George had thought long and hard about the phrase 'as long the cat lives' but had decided that the spirit of his promise to his dying mother included ensuring that no ill befell Pebbles while she was in his care. As a result he had looked after the cat diligently for two years, four months and three days after his mother's funeral until the vet had suggested it may be time to consider putting it down due to its advanced old age and poor vision. In truth the vet had simply been preparing the ground for what would become an inevitable requirement at some time in the future and was slightly taken aback at how quickly his advice was accepted by George. As a result of that sad act, George had lived happily and cat-free for almost six months after that.

Then one day he had returned to his house after a couple of pints at The Ranch to find a cat sitting in his favourite chair. It was a tortoiseshell-patterned beast with a luxurious coat straining to cover an extremely obese body. It also had a swollen eye as if it had come second in a recent territorial dispute. He tried to shoo it off his chair and it ignored him completely.

George was not an unkind man and although he did not like cats, his feelings did not extend to being cruel to them, so he sat down on the sofa to watch both the television and the cat. The cat watched him but not the television. After a relatively short period of time George started to find this uncomfortable for no good reason. He decided that some milk might distract the cat enough to get it to move into the kitchen. If he could close the door and trap it there it might head back out the cat flap later. If it did he would nail the damn thing shut as he had meant to sometime before. Like many things in George's life these days he hadn't quite got round to it yet.

"Here puss, puss," he said softly walking through to the kitchen and pouring the last of his milk into one of Pebbles' old dishes which he had stored in the pantry, hoping to never need again. He placed the dish on the floor and called on the cat again. Nothing happened. He walked through to the front room with the dish of milk in his hand and showed it to the cat. Again nothing happened. He passed it slowly in front of the cat's mouth, close enough for it to lick it with its tongue if it so chose. The cat stared at him, watching his every move but made no other movement.

After ten minutes or so George got bored and sat down again on the sofa to watch his favourite quiz show having first put the dish of milk back on the floor of the kitchen.

This pattern continued for a few tense days as George and the uninvited cat vied for possession of his favourite chair. No matter how closely George watched the cat he was unable to catch it leaving the front room and was therefore unable to eject it from his house.

A few days later George was trudging slowly up the hill towards his house with the two carrier bags of shopping banging against his legs in an annoying fashion as he did so. Ahead on a lamppost he noticed someone had placed an A4 size poster with a picture in the middle of it. He assumed from a distance that it was a poster for a local gig or perhaps a council threat of grievous retribution for anyone who didn't clean up their dog's poo. As he got closer though he noticed the picture was of a very overweight tortoiseshell cat.

Apparently it was called Vienna, was missing, and its owner loved it so much that she not only had a good recent photo of it but was also willing to pay £200 for its safe return. George looked at the picture carefully and recognised the unmistakable gaze of his current unwanted guest. He put down the shopping bags gently but they still spilled some of their contents onto the pavement. He reached for his mobile phone, typed in and saved the name and number. Carefully placing the phone back to its usual resting place in the back pocket of his jeans he gathered up the shopping and headed home at a brisker pace.

When he got there he put all of the frozen food into his freezer and the fresh items into his fridge. The rest of the shopping could wait he thought and made himself a cup of tea. Once it was ready he went to his favourite chair in the living room and sat down. After a couple of refreshing sips from his cup he pulled out his mobile phone and called the number from the poster.

"Hello, Coatshill 6998," said a mature well-spoken lady when the call was answered.

"Is that the lady who has lost her cat?" asked George in as professional and disinterested tone as he could manage.

"Yes it is, have you any news?" pleaded the voice at the other end of the line.

"I do indeed," said George casually. "I believe I have Vienna here."

"Where..? How..? Oh never mind! Are you sure it's her?" gasped the woman, overcome with emotion and relief.

"She certainly matches the picture on your wanted ad and there can't be many cats as fat as that."

There was a pause before a clearly offended voice corrected him. "She is big boned and very well nourished young man, not fat!"

'Bloody well nourished' thought George before saying, "It's just a technical term we use in the trade madam. No offence intended."

"What trade?" asked a still annoyed female voice.

George hadn't really thought that one through but, suddenly inspired, replied, "The Pet Recovery Business."

"You mean this is what you do for a living?"

George felt committed and added, "Yes, madam, I am a Cat Detective."

There was a pause at the other end of the line.

"Well then, when can you bring poor Vienna home? Or I could come and collect her."

"What's your address?" asked George, not keen on having a lady cat lover anywhere near his house.

"23, Pine Park; do you know it?"

"Yes, I could drop her off in an hour or so if that suited," said George judging it would take him about that time to walk to the address. "Will you have the reward money ready?"

"I can write you a cheque if that's what you mean," said Vienna's owner.

George sighed, "That will be grand Mrs….?"

"MISS Miller! And your name is..?"

"George Milne. I'll see you shortly."

George hung up and finished his tea. A cheque wasn't ideal but £200 was not bad for a few more scratches on his sofa and two tins of cat food.

Vienna had watched all of this activity with no sign of interest. She kept watching as George walked into the hall way and returned with a cat-carrier which had Pebbles written on the side. The sight of this and the fact that George had fully closed the door behind him seemed to ring warning bells in the cats head and she jumped down from the sofa with surprising speed for such a big boned and well-nourished animal.

George realised he hadn't been quick enough and made a lunge for Vienna. She was far too fast for him and managed to hide behind his sofa. He pulled it away from the wall with his left hand and held the cat carrier in his right hand. Again Vienna was too quick for him and hid under the table. George crouched down and tried to reach under the table to grab hold of her but again Vienna escaped and this time made it under his TV cabinet. This game of tig went on for half an hour or so with the cat using all the pieces of furniture to their maximum effect as hiding places. Eventually in sheer frustration, George grabbed a table cloth from a drawer and threw it like a net over Vienna when she made her next move. Trapped under the cloth the cat hissed and howled but couldn't escape. George opened up the cat-carrier and positioned it beside the table cloth which he had secured around the demented animal with his legs and arms. Reaching in he grabbed for the cat and after touching a selection of unpleasant parts and sustaining a number of scratches on his hand and arm he got a tight grip on her collar and yanked her roughly into the carrier, securing the door tightly behind her.

The cat carrier started to get heavy as he walked towards the address he had been given and he had to swap it from one arm to the other on a regular basis. Eventually he arrived at the house and walked up to the door. Before he could ring the bell the door flew open and Miss Miller appeared. She was a tiny lady of about 60 or so and could only have weighed about five stone fully dressed. Despite this she almost hoisted George up the three steps and into her house so that she could welcome Vienna home.

George placed the carrier on the carpet of the hallway and Miss Miller prised the door open. A far from happy Vienna allowed herself to be removed from the temporary prison and then endured an embarrassing tirade of kisses, hugs and gentle reprimands for being such a naughty pussy.

George genuinely felt like throwing up but managed to keep his stomach and feelings under control.

After what seemed like a lifetime Miss Miller looked at Vienna closely and noticed the swollen eye. She looked George up and down and noticed a series of scratches on his right arm.

Before she could ask any difficult questions George volunteered an explanation. "I found her having an altercation with a black Tom cat and had to pull them apart. Unfortunately the Tom cat gave me a bit of a hard time. Still, all in a day's work." George smiled.

"You poor man. You poor, brave man," said Miss Miller and she made a movement as if to take George's hand.

He managed to move out of range and lift his hand in a friendly way as if to say, 'It's nothing, really.'

Miss Miller stopped her advance towards him and still enthusing about his bravery made her way into the living room, still carrying a placid and smug looking Vienna.

George shuffled his feet, not really sure what to do next, but in fact did nothing. After a few minutes Miss Miller returned with a cheque in her hand.

"Here is your reward, young man, with a little extra for your troubles."

She handed George a cheque made out in his name for £300. He thanked her politely, told her she shouldn't have etc. but pocketed the cheque anyway and left.

Chapter Six

Although George had not become a great darts player he had become one of the gang who regularly played darts in The Ranch every Friday and some Sunday nights. It was a fairly diverse group but shared a common need for company on these two nights of the week for different reasons.

Willie Taylor worked as a technician in a local factory. He was as sharp as a razor but being about 50 or so had gone through school at a time when his dyslexia went unrecognised. Instead he tended to be branded by his teachers as lazy, slow, and always had comments like 'could do better' if he applied himself on his report card. As result he had left school with few qualifications and had gone to work initially at Franny's Bakery, working on the line. Rightly seeing no future there he had managed to get a job in a neighbouring coat-hanger factory. There his intelligence had been spotted and he had been trained up as a technician ensuring the aging machines kept churning out hangers, day and night without the expensive requirement to be replaced. His ability to keep the machines rolling made him popular with the management while his quick wit and dry sense of humour made him popular with the rest of the workforce on the shop floor.

Old Jock was a regular in The Ranch and worked in the same factory as Willie. He was as slow-witted as Willie was fast. It could take anywhere from five minutes to four days longer for Jock to get a joke than the rest of the group. If the joke was at his expense he would generally take it in good part, especially if Willie had come up with it. As a result he was the perfect straight man for Willie.

Gordon Beaton was a 22-year-old student of computer design at Strathclyde University in nearby Glasgow, still lived at home with his parents and commuted daily for his studies. He was tall and skinny and had a girlfriend called Jenny who he religiously spent every Saturday night with. To ensure that she had no reason to believe he was ready to settle down, Gordon went out with the boys on Fridays and Sundays. Having no real friends from university living nearby, any boys would do, which made The Ranch darts players an ideal group to join. He took a lot of stick from the others who referred to him as 'the boy' etc., but he could give as good as he got and the banter was all done in friendship.

Ray Lindsay was the only one of the group to take darts seriously, and in fairness was the best player there. He was a brickie with a local building firm and although he was slightly less than average height he was built like the proverbial brick shit-house. He had a set of darts that had been very expensive when new, although this had not been recently. He could add and subtract numbers between 501 and zero in a way that could have got him on TV. Any other academic studies defeated him but between those numbers his mental agility was unsurpassed in any company.

Another occasional member of the dart playing group was a man in his late 30s called Callum. He no doubt had a surname but nobody ever knew it. He was a friendly type of guy and often bought a round of drinks for whoever he was playing darts with, with no expectation of getting one bought for him in return. He drove a white transit van which he sometimes left parked outside if he had drunk more than his customary two beers, which was a rare occurrence. He never mentioned specifically what he did for a living but whatever it was it appeared to pay well. Callum dressed in smart but casual clothes which suggested large price tags. He would talk in general terms of having to visit Edinburgh, Glasgow or a whole range of smaller Scottish towns, giving no details of why, although he had a vast store of funny stories of incidents which had occurred during his travels. All in all the other darts players would look forward to his visits as a welcome break from the usual routine.

On one of the regular sessions, George's mobile phone rang unexpectedly and he answered it with a cautious, "Hello."

"Hello, is that the Cat Detective?" a mature female voice enquired, loud enough for some of the other players to hear it.

"What?" said George still wondering why his phone had rung at all for the first time in two weeks.

"Mr Milne, the Cat Detective?" the voice persisted.

"This is George Milne," said George still a little bit confused.

"Good, I want you to find my cat. It's been missing for over a week now and I'm frantic with worry."

George was about to explain that he was not in fact a cat detective when she added, "I'll pay your fee just to look for Snowy."

An idea formed in George's mind and he replied, "I could maybe take on the case on top of my current workload but I can make no promises if it's been missing for a full week"

"Oh thank you, thank you," said a relieved voice at the other end. "My name is Ms Johnson and I live in Willow Way at number 17. Do you know where that is?"

George knew it well and promised a grateful Ms Johnson that he would call in to get the details around 11 o'clock the next morning if his other case commitments allowed. He ended the call and looked round at the other darts players in The Ranch who were all staring at him and smiling or giggling.

"What?" he asked.

They just smiled and restarted the game.

Chapter Seven

As a rule Frankie Cook or Wacky Frank didn't go out much at the weekends. Instead he stayed in the top floor tenement which served as his headquarters, and directed the busy days when everyone seemed to want to buy drugs of some kind. None of it ever made it into his flat and only enough of the financial proceeds arrived there to pay his personal day to day running costs. His entire business was conducted at arm's length by his lieutenants, enforcers and below them an army of victims at the bottom of the food chain. When he did go out it was usually early in the week on a Tuesday or Monday after business had been largely concluded within his empire and the money divvied up. On these occasions he would usually nip into his local pub, The Ranch, for a few pints when it was quiet and would then go on to Coatshill's only nightclub, The Magic Lantern, or into Glasgow to one of the more fashionable clubs there.

He liked The Ranch though, for a number of reasons. His occasional presence there meant that none of his clients ever went in. It was usually fairly quiet and served a good pint. He also knew a few of the regulars from his school days and managed to persuade himself that they were all old pals together. Truth was he had never really had any pals at school, but those who knew him and drank in The Ranch were smart enough not to point this out to him. They also appreciated Frankie's generous rounds of drinks without thinking too much about where the money had come from. So it was on the nights that Frankie popped into The Ranch for a few beers with his old buddies that an uneasy atmosphere of false relaxation would persist until he headed off to a club. Frankie never talked business on such occasions and those present would make a point of talking about anything but drugs to keep things jolly and bright.

As a result of this patronage, The Ranch was one of the most peaceful pubs in the town. When Frankie was there, everybody behaved. If anyone stepped out of line when he wasn't there, they would suffer as soon as he heard about it. The regular barmaid, Janine McGovern, was perfectly capable of sorting out most trouble before it came to anything, but it did no harm whatsoever to be able to mention Frankie's name if people persisted in giving her or any of her locals any lip.

One of the main reasons Frankie frequented The Ranch though was because of Janine's 19-year-old daughter Rosie. Rosie was beautiful in a film star, Miss World, fashion model way that meant she stood out among the other women in Coatshill like a sore thumb. Or perhaps they were all sore thumbs next to her. Either way, once you saw her you never forgot the moment, and like every other regular Frankie was smitten. Rosie would work some Saturday shifts with her mother to help out and regularly worked Tuesday nights which was her mother's only day off most weeks.

Thus it was that on a regular basis Frankie Cook would try his hardest to sweet talk Rosie into going out with him to a club or indeed on a date of any kind. It was also due to this regular pattern of working that George Milne had never met Rosie.

Janine McGovern had worked at The Ranch for as long as most of its regulars could remember. She had moved to Coatshill from Glasgow as a single mother with her daughter Rosie to make a fresh start. She never discussed her past in detail with any of the clientele of the pub but over the years they gained the impression that she had split from a violent and abusive husband after reaching breaking point, and that as part of the new arrangement he was banned by the courts from setting eyes on his wife or daughter ever again. From fear of legal retribution or from lack of interest, as far as anyone could make out, he had never bothered to try.

Janine herself was a good looking woman who kept her looks as she gently aged behind the bar. None of the regulars had ever succeeded in going out with her although most had tried their hand. In the end, after her first few years there, everyone concerned fell into an arrangement whereby any flirting was restricted to friendly banter on both sides. Clearly it was a case of once bitten twice shy.

She was good at her job, looked after her regulars well and welcomed everyone across the threshold with a smile. The absentee landlord of The Ranch, who owned several pubs in and around Glasgow, rarely visited, knowing that it was one pub he didn't need to worry about. It was busy, always returned a profit and there never appeared to be any money or drink going astray. To all intents and purposes then, it was Janine's pub.

If Janine was a conscientious publican, she was a devoted mother who watched over her daughter Rosie with an unfailing protective eye. Whatever feelings she had toward the father of her child, her love for her daughter was without bounds. Rosie was immaculately turned out for school every day with everything she needed to succeed and be happy there. Rosie was not in any way spoiled but always had enough of the latest toys and, later as she grew older, fashions to be popular with her contemporaries and to fit in. Her time spent in The Ranch after school gave her experience of talking to people in a natural way and she soon learned how to charm even the dourest of regulars into a smile or the gift of a packet of crisps.

She loved her mother dearly and made no real distinction in her own eyes of any separation between the staff flat or the public bar in terms of her home. If she missed her father she never said so and perhaps having dozens of surrogate fathers at her beck and call helped.

Janine appeared to have dedicated this part of her life to raising Rosie and allowing nobody else to enter her affections. Deep down she had clearly shelved her own chances of romance until her daughter was grown up and had found somebody to take over the responsibility for looking after her for life. Till then Janine would run the bar to the best of her considerable ability and focus on her daughter's happiness. Any potential love interest for Janine in the meantime could come and go unfulfilled.

Over the years, the regulars of The Ranch had watched Janine's daughter Rosie grow up almost as if she was a child of their own. When Janine had started work there, Rosie had been seven and came from her primary school to The Ranch each day and sat down to do her homework in the booth nearest the bar. She was a bright and cheerful child who chatted incessantly to the customers who in turn spoiled her with drinks of cola, sweets and crisps from behind the bar. If Janine had allowed them to, they would have overfed Rosie to the point of clinical obesity by the time she reached High School. Instead, all treats were restricted on a daily basis and when punters insisted on buying more junk for Rosie than she was allowed that day, Janine would thank them and tell them it would form part of the contents of her lunch box or morning snack the following day. It rarely did as Janine was very careful about what her daughter ate, often returning the snack to the shelf and pocketing the cost before cashing up.

As Rosie grew up and went on to the local High School, many of her friends from The Ranch watched with pride as she grew in to a beautiful young woman. Many found themselves struggling with feelings that were far from paternal too as she blossomed into one of Coatshill's greatest beauties long before leaving school. She and her mother would have the customary arguments that only mothers and daughters have over what it was permissible to wear and what was a reasonable curfew time on school nights. The regulars at The Ranch would join in, always on Rosie's side, until her mother inevitably laid down the law with a look that threatened exclusion to anyone who disagreed.

Rosie started to work sometimes, collecting the empty glasses from tables and in due course, as the law permitted, she would work occasional shifts. She was as popular with the regulars when she did this as she had ever been and was easily able to control behaviour, knowing sufficient of them for years to shame them if they stepped out of line.

On one weekend, during her final year at High School, she went to 'T in the Park' with a group of school friends. After two weeks away she returned with a new friend called Carol who was every bit as beautiful as Rosie herself. The two girls appeared inseparable and shared the spare room in the staff flat occupied by Janine. As the weeks went by, the smarter of the locals realised that they were in fact a very happy couple. Willie Taylor was probably the first to catch on and Jock would have been the last as usual if Frankie Cook had not been blinded by his obsession with Rosie.

Carol was a free spirit who had studied at Art College and travelled much of the world, despite the fact that she was still in her early twenties, only slightly older than Rosie. She would occasionally come into The Ranch, usually when Rosie was working, but even then was happier out and about looking for inspiration for her next art work. Her parents were relatively well off and had funded her bohemian lifestyle to the full. She had travelled to Rome and Paris to improve her technique and then travelled through Asia, Australia and New Zealand before working her way from the southern tip of South America to the home of wealthy cousins in Canada over a six month period. Along the way she had experimented with drink, drugs, boys and girls, producing pictures inspired by all of them as she went. The best of these were shipped home while others adorned the walls of bars and restaurants around the globe. Her late teenage years and early twenties had been one long adventure as she grew into a worldly wise and relatively talented artist at her parents' expense. Returning to her flat in Edinburgh, conveniently owned by her parents, she became listless and bored. She was so young and had experienced so many things that she was not quite sure what was left for her. Then she met Rosie. It was love at first sight and with it came the chance to experience something which had escaped Carol until then: The real world.

Rosie had grown up in a very different world to Carol, where every penny was counted and only spent reluctantly and wisely. Rosie had worked part-time almost all her life, helping her mother in the pub clearing tables or serving during functions, not because it was fun or exciting as Carol's Saturday job in Harvey Nichols had been, but because she had had to in order to have any money of her own.

The one person who was blind to the love between Rosie and Carol was Frankie Cook. He was obsessed with her and would spend hours trying to chat her up. At first she would turn down his advances with humour and good grace but as he became more and more besotted with her she realised he was not going to take the hint. He slowly became more insistent that she go out with him on a date. How could anyone refuse him? he seemed to say each time she turned him down. Then he became a little bit threatening as he tired of her refusals. In the end she decided to come clean about her sexuality, assuming that that would put him off once and for all.

It didn't.

"It's just a phase you young girls go through," he said in response. "You'll get over it. Especially after you've been out with a real man, who has shown you a good time. You could even bring your pal Carol if you like, make it a threesome," he added with a wink.

This type of conversation became a recurring theme for Rosie on the nights she covered for her mother. Eventually they became a nightmare as Frankie's threats became more sinister. It came to a head when he told her that either she went out with him the following week or he would make sure nobody looked at her ever again, male or female.

Rosie was scared and with good reason. All her contemporaries knew Frankie by reputation or in person and knew what he was capable of. She confided in Janine, who promised to sort something out, though in the meantime it would be best if Rosie laid low somewhere safe.

Chapter Eight

Wacky Frank Cook's younger sister Evelyn had been born four years after him. From an early stage at school it was clear to her teachers that she struggled with the standard curriculum but because she appeared to try very hard and made some progress each year she was kept in mainstream education all her days. In her first few years at school she was the butt of teasing and bullying, but as her older brother and his lifetime buddy Willie McBride came to dominate the school playground, she found she was generally left well alone. She would play occasionally with other girls in her age group but never had any close friends.

She often appeared to be in a world of her own but as she seemed to be a happy enough girl and was never disruptive, her teachers left her largely to her own devices. For Evelyn, school formed a pleasant break from the violence and misery of her home life.

Her father was a violent drunk who both sexually and physically abused Evelyn and her mother on an almost daily basis. Her mother escaped into a world of alcoholic relief. Her bother Frankie had been badly beaten from the moment he was born and as he grew older found his escape in staying out of the family home as much as possible. In his later primary school years he would often not return home till both his father and mother were lying comatose on their bed or on the seating in their front room. At that stage he got used to tidying away any lit cigarettes, putting a guard in front of the fire if anyone had managed to light it and then checking that his sister had survived the day. He would quietly slip into the room they shared and whisper, "You awake, Evie?" It was a name only Frankie used and it made her feel safe.

Almost without exception she would still be wide awake; too scared to sleep till her brother was home and could offer some sort of protection, even if it was only an alternative target for her father's blows. He would dress any obvious wounds and give her any food he had stolen or been given by Willie's mother and then lie on top of her covers with his arm around her until she drifted off to sleep in some world where hopefully their father could not reach her. At these times Frankie would promise her that someday he would make a home for the two of them and their mother, which would be a safe and happy place for them all.

"Will there be animals?" she would ask.

"Of course," he would reassure her. "What kind of animals would you like?"

She would think for a minute or two and ream off a list. "Cats, dogs, monkeys, zebras and giraffes. Promise me Frankie that you'll do that one day and I'll be safe and happy!"

"I'll get as many of them as I can, and I swear on my own life I'll do that for you, Evie," he would promise her as her list tailed off into restless sleep.

The following day, if they were lucky the two children would manage to get dressed, have breakfast if there was food in the house and leave for school before their father awoke. If they were unlucky he would wake first and wake them with the swinging of his belt.

Their mother would sometimes make it out of her stupor before they left and would dissolve in to a tearful apology for the previous day, promising never to drink again and to be a better mother. She may even have meant it at the time but by that evening, after brutal retribution from her husband for imagined slights, she would have consumed a bottle of vodka before the kids got home, thus escaping again into oblivion and leaving them to their fate.

Their mother, who had died relatively young from a combination of domestic violence and alcohol abuse, had made Frankie swear on at least four potential death beds that he would look after Evelyn whatever happened, when she could not. While Frankie was happy enough to kill, maim or beat up anybody in his day to day business affairs, he could deny his mother nothing. As a result of her dying wish he had taken on responsibility for his sister when his mother finally died at the age of 49 from liver failure. This was approximately five years after his father had died from a terminal case of compassion fatigue on Frankie's part one night, which combined a badly beaten up mother and sister, a violent and unrepentantly drunken father, a quiet area of Glasgow's former shipbuilding glory and an ever loyal Willie McBride. Frankie did not in any way mourn the passing of his drunken and abusive father but he had struggled to come to terms with the death of his mother.

When he eventually returned home that evening and told Evelyn that their father was gone for good and would never bother her or their mother again, Evelyn looked at him and said, "Thanks Frankie, you're the best."

Evelyn Cook lived with her brother for a few years after their mother died and seemed to make progress towards some kind of normal life. Through a committed social worker and personal determination she got a job at Franny's Bakery and at first seemed to thrive. Her duties were kept deliberately simple but on the basis that the local authority covered all the costs of her employment there, Franny's were happy to have an extra pair of hands in production, especially if they were free.

Franny's Bakery had been a local institution in Coatshill for over 150 years. Franny herself had started the enterprise in the town's Cadzow Street with a small inheritance and, by the time of her death in 1903 had built it up to a chain of ten retail outlets. Her two children inherited it and built on the strong foundations laid by their mother. They added a further five shops and a centralised manufacturing unit which took advantage of the speed of delivery afforded by vans powered by the new internal combustion engine. Unusually for many family businesses, two further generations had shown the interest and business acumen to grow the business further, so that it survived and flourished in good times and bad, providing full and part time employment to several hundred people in and around the town. They took pride in being a family business and boasted that they had never made people redundant, even in the worst of times. This ensured the loyal support of many local residents and this in turn helped them to weather the various economic storms over the years.

They were famous for many of their products and rightly so. Each shop displayed copies of prize certificates they had won for all manner of cakes, buns and breads. They produced traditional loaves of all shapes and sizes, including the uniquely Scottish plain loaf but they were also quick to spot new markets and now turned out Ciabattas, Nan breads and Gluten -free bread for both retail and restaurant customers. They were very active in providing outside catering for all manner of functions and organisations, including the local authority. They also had a specialist department which made wedding cakes to order and a catalogue was available in each outlet for happy couples to seek inspiration for their big day. Only the best of the workers got to work in this prestigious department and competition was fierce when vacancies arose.

For her part, Evelyn took a pride in being on time and with her cleanliness. She made some friends on the line who would include her in their conversations, which usually centred round popular television programmes or men; their own or other people's. Evelyn would smile and laugh along with them, never really sure what was going on but loving the company of other women and the security that it brought.

She was provided with training in the different departments before ending up on the production line. The office area was a mystery to her so her planned three weeks there was curtailed to two days but she showed promise in the department that made specialist cakes for weddings and birthdays – so much so that she was almost given a permanent place there, such was her skill with icing cream. Only her spelling let her down. In the end though, she went back to the line and was happy enough there.

It was while she was spending time in each of the departments that she came to the attention of Richard Pettigrew, a junior member of the sales department. Evelyn was a good looking girl and would have been noticed by most men who set eyes on her. Richard was a rather lonely 25-year-old who still lived with his parents and had had little luck with the girls in his life to date. This had made him somewhat shy and as a result he found himself drawn to Evelyn, who had no sarcasm or artistry in her dealings with men. They spoke during her brief stint in the office and Richard managed to time his breaks and lunches to coincide with hers as often as he could. She liked his attentions and he loved her simplicity, natural gentleness and beauty.

Frankie had enough clients amongst the staff at Franny's to know about Richard's attentions early on. He asked Evelyn about their conversations and what she thought about Richard when she came home each day. At first he had been dead against Evelyn having anything to do with any man but there seemed no harm in what they talked about from what he could ascertain.

Despite a few of Richard's colleagues having a word to the wise, pointing out that Evelyn was Wacky

Frank's sister he persisted. Eventually he plucked up the courage to ask her out. As a neutral first venue he asked if she fancied going to a football match with him. She was thrilled at the thought of a proper date but said she would have to ask her brother first.

Frankie was cautious but agreed on the condition that Richard had her home within 30 minutes of full time and that it didn't involve a game with either Rangers or Celtic.

The next day Evelyn told Richard that Frankie had agreed. She had forgotten what the conditions were but had remembered that her brother wanted a word with him before they went out together.

On the allotted Saturday Richard had appeared at number 10 Woodend Walk in the red and white stripes of Coatshill's finest, with a spare scarf for Evelyn. Willie McBride had shown him into the front room where Frankie was waiting. For as long he could remember Frankie had felt a protective duty towards his sister. Initially out of necessity as they grew up with their father in the house and then as their mother became less able and died, he had taken on the role of parent or guardian automatically. His instinctive mistrust of anyone showing interest in his sister had been tempered by the realisation that he might not always be there to look after her. Indeed, one bad day at the office and he might disappear without a trace from her life for ever. He was therefore more amenable to the idea of Evelyn settling down with someone else than he might otherwise have been.

This Richard was no hero but Frankie knew for an indisputable fact that he didn't do drugs. That was a good start. Richard's parents were hard working religious people who provided an extra safeguard to Evelyn's involvement with him. All in all, it might just prove to be an acceptable arrangement but first Frankie had to explain the basic ground rules of dating his sister. This took the form of a 15 minute briefing about what would happen to anyone who hurt his kid sister in any way shape or form. At the end of it a rather shaken looking Richard collected Evelyn from the hall of the flat and took her out to her first ever football match.

Evelyn came home, on time, full of stories to tell her brother. She had little understanding of the rules of the game but the crowds and the atmosphere had left her breathless. She went on and on about it that night till Frankie was bored rigid with the detail, but he was pleased to see his sister happy for once.

The weeks went by and Evelyn spent more and more time with Richard. Frankie spent less and less time worrying about it and soon took it for granted. On one occasion, he even took up the invitation from Richard's parents to have Sunday lunch with them.

The Pettigrew's may have regarded it as the most bizarre Sunday lunch ever but Frankie found it reassuring to meet them and confirm they were regular folks. Richard didn't say too much but that too was a plus in Frankie's eyes. Frankie noticed that Richard wore a ring with 999 on it and through a series of pointed questions quickly reassured himself that he wasn't a policeman or similar. It took a day or two for him to realise that it in fact read 666, the number of the beast, but by then Frankie's mind was busy on other more important matters. During the meal, Willie McBride sat outside the whole time in Frankie's Land Rover Discovery.

"Would your friend not like to come in and have a bite to eat?" Mrs Pettigrew asked on more than one occasion.

"No chance, he's working," replied Frankie.

"But he must be starving," she continued, not clear what work could be done from a parked Land Rover on a Sunday morning, even with a mobile phone constantly applied to one's ear.

"The bastard's fat enough," replied Frankie smiling at his own joke. That pretty much ended that line of conversation from Mrs P.

They only asked Frankie once about what he did for a living and again, uncomfortable with the language he used to suggest exactly how much of their business it was, tried to make small talk only, from then on.

In truth they were pleased and a little surprised that Richard had finally found himself a girlfriend. Evelyn wasn't their ideal choice of daughter-in-law material but she was sweet, pretty and gentle. Before she appeared on the scene, Richard had spent most of his spare time in his room on his computer, a pastime both parents viewed as unhealthy for a number of reasons. Mrs Pettigrew had once taken her son a mug of coffee and had gone into his bedroom without knocking. He appeared to be watching a film but it was like no film she had ever watched with her husband. A young Japanese girl appeared to be tied to an old fashioned Gym Horse and was being beaten with sticks by an older man. That was all she had caught before Richard changed the image on the screen and berated her for not knocking on his door before entering the room. She had later discussed what she had seen with her husband who promised to talk to his son but had never quite got round to it.

Now Richard had his first proper girlfriend and his parents both felt this was the start of a much healthier time in their son's life. As a result they were prepared to overlook any shortcomings on Evelyn's part and her rather worrying brother. All they wanted was what was best for their only son Richard.

After the Sunday lunch with the Pettigrews, Frankie largely left Evelyn's welfare to them whenever she was not in the flat at Woodend Walk. He assumed that if she was at their house or out with Richard she would be safe. He assumed wrong.

One weekend after Evelyn and Richard had been going out for six months or so and she had stayed at the Pettigrews' house on two prior occasions, she informed Frankie that she would again be staying over. Frankie and Willie were busy preparing for a critical business meeting at the time but Frankie put his shotgun down for a second and stared at his sister.

"Are you happy, Evie?" he asked her.

"Yes Frankie," she replied, "Very."

He just nodded and went on with his preparations unaware that Mr and Mrs Pettigrew were away for the weekend and did not know that Evelyn was invited round.

That night Frankie and Willie had some difficulties with negotiations and he did not return till midday on the Monday. When they did, Frankie found Evelyn sitting stock still on the sofa watching daytime TV when she should have been at work. She didn't turn to say hello. In fact she didn't acknowledge his arrival at all, even when he called through to her. Immediately he recognised her coping mode from years before when their father had still been alive and rushed through to her. When he saw her face, bruised and with a shiny black eye, he gently but firmly, held her in his arms.

"Who did this to you?" he asked her softly, masking the anger he felt welling up inside.

She did not reply.

"Was it Richard?" he asked and she nodded her head.

"What did he do to you?"

At last she looked round at her brother and he saw the familiar old lost look had returned to her eyes.

"What dad did," she said. "I tried to stop him though and he tied me and hurt my back."

With that she turned back to the television having said all she would say. Frankie turned her round slightly on the couch and gently raised her blouse at the back. He could see vicious welts on the small area he had exposed and indications that they continued both up the way and down. Evelyn was sitting on a cushion which confirmed his suspicions. He released the bottom of her blouse, leant over and kissed her cheek.

"He'll never do that again, I promise you," he whispered in her ear, then stood up and walked through to the kitchen with a face of stone. Frankie was as angry as it was possible to be. He was angry with Richard fucking Pettigrew, it was true. He was angry with Richard's parents with no real reason. But above all else he was angry with himself for letting his kid sister down. He had promised to protect her and keep her safe and he had failed on both counts. Somebody was going to pay for the suffering inflicted on his sister. Someone was going to atone for what happened and for Frankie having his eye off the ball. That someone was going to be Richard Pettigrew.

"What's up?" asked Willie who had just sat down and put the kitchen television on but, recognising the look on Frankie's face, immediately switched it off again.

"That bastard beat Evelyn, and worse. He's just killed himself though." There was a look of utter rage and hatred in Frankie's face that worried even Willie.

"We'll get him after work and take him for a ride into the country," said Willie.

"No," said Frankie. "It's too close to home; we'll get collared for it. Anyway that would be too good for him. I'll get Spider to deal with him and we'll both have alibis."

Willie nodded deciding that a few hours with Stevie 'Spider' Webb given carte blanche, would be about as bad an end as he could imagine.

That evening Willie sat in the flat at Woodend Walk, kept company by Evelyn and one of her colleagues from Franny's, Fiona Greer. Fiona had been surprised to receive a phone call from Frankie asking if she would visit Evelyn that night but he explained she had missed work that day and was quite upset, so Fiona had agreed. Apparently Evelyn had asked for her by name. Taking that as a compliment and being quite fond of Evelyn, she had finished work early and made her way to the flat by half past four. Frankie had let her in and explained he had to go out but thanked her and said Willie McBride would be there if Evelyn had any problems. Fiona was a sweet and kind natured girl. She nodded and smiled at Frankie, who she knew little about and assured him that she was just the person to cheer Evelyn up. The fact that Fiona was the daughter of a local Police Sergeant also made her the perfect alibi for Willie.

Frankie made his way straight to The Ranch, arriving at exactly 4.45. A fact Janine would have remembered as he asked her the time when he arrived, having apparently left his watch at home that day. He stayed in the pub till closing time and indeed well after 11 o'clock, having drunk only a few pints, played darts and spoken to everyone present that night.

Richard Pettigrew left work shortly after 5 p.m. and was last seen at about 5.20 by a colleague as he turned into Burnblae Lane, which was a short cut to the High

Street on his way home. Burnblae Lane was a relatively short and rarely used path between two tenement blocks with side entrances to both and to the areas where the bins were parked. Nobody saw him exit the other end of the lane. Nobody that is, except Stevie 'Spider' Webb.

The day Frankie met Stevie he felt like he had won a watch. Stevie was the perfect enforcer for anyone in the drugs business. He had no emotions of any kind, other than seeming to enjoy inflicting pain. He would carry out any instructions to the letter and was not afraid of anything. He had no limits in terms of violence and regarded delivering a brutal beating as one of the perks of the job. He had 'hate' tattooed on both sets of knuckles, which pretty much summed up his work ethos. Soon after he started working for Frankie the number of people in arrears with their payments plummeted. His reputation went before him and the mention of a visit by Spider was enough to make most debtors cough up, whatever it took. As Frankie used to say to Willie, "Spider is the psychopath's psychopath," and Frankie knew what he was talking about.

They had first met when Spider delivered a large batch of heroin from Liverpool. He had initially seemed an unremarkable courier. Not very big, no conversation skills and none of the flash clothing or jewellery that Frankie might have expected. Indeed, the transaction might have come and gone almost unnoticed in the general scheme of things, had a crisis of sorts not arisen during his visit. While Frankie checked the merchandise and Willie watched Spider count the payment for it, Frankie's phone went off.

"What?" asked Frankie irritably.

A raised voice at the other end of the line went into overdrive. Both Spider and Willie stopped what they were doing to listen. The voice at the other end of the line went on for some time till Frankie cut it short.

"Shut the fuck up. Tell him I'm coming over myself with Willie and he better have the money when we get there." Then he looked at Willie. "Hurry up Willie, Shanksy's three grand short. I've told that useless bastard Bob we'll sort it ourselves. After we've sorted Shanksy, you go and see Bob. Tell him he's fuck all use to me if wankers like Shanksy aren't scared of him."

Willie nodded and turned back to Spider expecting him to finish counting the money. Instead he put all of the notes into the daysack he had brought with him for the purpose. Then he turned to Frankie.

"I'm sure it's all there," he said. "Mind if I tag along?"

Frankie and Willie were a bit surprised but nodded and they headed off in Frankie's car to pay Shanksy a visit. They arrived soon afterwards at a council house in the last scheme in Coatshill before the road headed into the countryside in the direction of Ayrshire. Frankie and Willie jumped out of the vehicle and Spider offered to cover the back door. The other two kicked in the front door of the house which had the look of a door regularly kicked in rather than opened using the handle. Once inside they pushed past a woman in a shell suit who tried to block their way and rushed through to the front room which was empty and on into the kitchen. It too was empty but here was a freshly made mug of coffee on the work top. Seeing the back door was open Frankie and Willie rushed over to it and out into the back garden. There, amongst a host of discarded furniture and rusting white goods they found Shanksy lying on the ground with blood streaming from his nose and mouth. Spider was standing over the considerably larger man with a look of murder in his eyes.

He turned to watch the other two arrive before returning his gaze to the bloodied figure on the ground.

"I think you should pay Frankie what you owe him, or I'll take you home with me to Liverpool for a bit of fun," he said in a calm and utterly emotionless tone.

"Okay, okay," shouted Shanksy. "I've got two grand stashed here. I can get the rest by Friday."

Spider looked at Frankie who nodded and Shanksy was allowed to stand up and re-enter the house. The three watched him as he took a bundle of notes from a biscuit jar on one of the higher shelves in the kitchen with his hands alternating between shaking and wiping blood from his face.

"There, that's all I've got here. Honest. I'll bring you the rest on Friday."

Frankie stared him in the eyes and decided he was telling the truth.

"I want it handed over to Willie before midday or we'll be back."

With that, he grabbed the bundle of notes and led the way back to the car. Once they were all inside, he peeled off a generous number of the notes and handed them to Spider.

"Thanks for your help there mate."

Spider declined to take the money. "You're okay. I enjoyed that. Any more work going? I'm bored with The Pool."

Frankie looked at Willie, who had been impressed with how quickly and how effectively Spider had floored Shanksy, and nodded his agreement.

"Well if you fancy taking over Bob's patch that could be helpful."

"Show me where he lives on our way back to my car and I'll sort him out after I've delivered the cash to Scouse central. I feel a change of scenery coming on."

They drove a long route back and stopped a hundred yards along the road from Bob's house. Once Spider was happy that he could find the right house again they drove off.

"What does Bob look like?" he asked.

"Big fat bastard with sideburns, can't miss him," replied Willie.

Two days later Bob went missing and Spider took over money collection duties where Bob had left off.

———————————————

When Spider received a call from Frankie asking him to carry out a special favour, he was all ears. Frankie was sure that the police were paying particular attention to him at that time or he would have sorted this issue out for himself. Frankie explained how personally upset he was with Richard Pettigrew and why. The next best thing when it came to personal revenge was to know that the victim had fallen foul of Spider with a licence to kill, slowly. Spider accepted the job with a cheery, "This one's on the house."

A photo of Richard was sent to Spider's phone, memorised and then deleted. In the remaining hours before the daytime workers left Franny's, Spider made his preparations, filling the boot of his car with a variety of ropes, restraints, power tools and a blowtorch . This would be a night he would remember for a long time he thought to himself as he waited with anticipation in the shadows of Burnblae Lane.

When Richard didn't return home from work for his tea that evening his parents were immediately worried. He had often gone for a few pints after work with his friends and colleagues and was selfish enough not to inform his mother on these occasions. She regularly kept his food warm in the oven for a while and eventually covered it for reheating late that night or even as a lunch for work the next day.

Richard had even stayed over at a friend's house on two previous occasions after drinking too much, again without thinking to let his parents know.

As a result it wasn't until the next morning when the Human Resources department of Franny's phoned to ask why Richard hadn't either turned up for work or phoned in sick that his mother thought something might be amiss. At that point though, she became concerned and started to phone round some of his regular haunts, such as they were. She started with Evelyn but was informed by her, then Frankie, that Richard hadn't been round there for a few days. Neither of the two pubs he frequented had seen him the night before and Franny's phoned back to confirm that he had not gone out or gone home with any other employees from there. They said they were genuinely concerned and would phone if any further information came to light.

Mrs Pettigrew decided after phoning her husband and asking him to come home from work that she should inform the police. As Richard was 25 years old the police didn't regard it as a priority but did eventually send an officer round that evening. The policewoman took down the details, reassuring the Pettigrews that it was probably nothing to worry about. Her attitude changed however when she asked for details about Richard's girlfriend. On discovering that he was dating Wacky Frank Cook's sister she looked round with sudden interest.

"So they have been going out for a while?" she checked. "Had they met her brother Francis Cook? He had actually been round for Sunday lunch? What had they talked about?"

The questions continued for some time all aimed at pinning down their knowledge and dealings with Evelyn's brother. After a full 15 minutes of questioning the policewoman excused herself, went outside and radioed in to the station that the routine missing person had turned out to be the boyfriend of Frankie Cook's sister and that his parents believed they might have had an argument over the weekend.

A duty inspector took charge of the enquiry as officers were dispatched to interview Frankie, Willie McBride and Evelyn. The inspector personally re-interviewed the Pettigrews, which scared the bejesus out of them. Frankie and Willie were brought in separately for questioning. Evelyn was interviewed at 10 Woodend Walk by specialist female officers. Once all the statements were taken, they were studied and all alibis were checked out. Janine and four regulars from The Ranch confirmed Frankie's whereabouts the evening before while a rather embarrassed Fiona Greer confirmed that she had spent the whole evening at Frankie's flat with his sister until almost midnight when Frankie came home and Willie McBride had been there all the time. Fiona's father was livid but was immediately removed from the team working the case.

The following day Richard's mutilated body was discovered in an unused warehouse in Glasgow by children who had broken into it in order to cycle out of the rain. His death had been slow and extremely painful and showed all the signs that he had been kidnapped and killed by a sexual psychopath. In addition to all the other injuries, his ring finger was missing along with the distinctive 666 ring his mother had described. An unusually squeamish coroner concluded murder with a time of death likely to be somewhere in the middle of the evening he had gone missing. Inspector Menzies knew that somehow Frankie was behind it but he and his right hand man Willie McBride had cast iron alibis. The case remained open but after exhaustive inquiries the bulk of the team were pulled off it and reassigned to other work.

Chapter Nine

George had taken to walking around the streets of Coatshill on a regular basis and would sometimes bump into one of his clients. He felt that in some ways he was indeed looking for all the missing cats. Not necessarily in a specific or methodical manner, but in a general sense of being aware of any cats he encountered as he went.

The walking had replaced an earlier attempt at salving his conscience over collecting money from distraught cat owners without doing anything in return. It had started after he returned from The Ranch one night slightly the worse for wear. In his befuddled state he realised that the night times were really the times the missing cats were most likely to be out and about. If he could tempt them into his house via the cat flap he could possibly capture them. After all, he somehow managed to convince himself, he had managed that with Vienna. He decided to put this plan into action that very night without further delay and without waiting to sober up. A quick tour of the house produced everything he felt he would need. He had a packet of 'Dreamies' cat treats, a bowl of cat food, his file of photographs of the current missing cats and a water pistol filled with cold water. He moved one of his kitchen chairs to a strategically placed location to the side of his back door where the cat flap was located. Then he went back outside and laid a trail of Dreamies from his front gate to his back door. He then placed the bowl of cat food at the furthest corner away from the door and sat down in the chair with the file in one hand and the water pistol in the other. If one of his clients' cats took the bait he would block its escape. If any other cat entered his house through the cat flap, he would dowse it with cold water to make sure it didn't try to establish squatters' rights.

Thus prepared he waited on the chair for ten minutes before falling fast asleep, waking in the early hours of the morning with a stiff neck. The cat food had gone from the bowl and when he checked outside, the Dreamies had all mysteriously disappeared too. After having a drink of water from the pistol he staggered off to bed. When he again woke up at half past nine he made a coffee and decided regular patrolling of the surrounding streets might be a better option.

George had been enjoying his walks more and more as the weather improved and he felt as if he was at least making some effort for the money he took from his clients. Clients was an impressive term for five lonely and distraught old ladies (two of whom were in fact married and one of whom was under 30, but George viewed them all collectively as lonely old

77

ladies like his mother had been). Why else would they have a cat?

He got to know all the roads round his house like the back of his hand: Hawthorn Hill, Willow Way and all the other roads in the area which had been given alliterative names, for whatever reason. The main exception to this was Abernethy Boulevard which was named after William Abernethy MBE, a former councillor and provost of Coatshill who had served the people of the area selflessly for over 30 years, without once being caught or even accused of corruption. That was no small feat in the days of his service to the community and pictures hung throughout the town of him planting trees and opening the occasional new building. Mainly though, they were of him planting trees. Not just laying the first ceremonial sod but sleeves rolled up, digging and placing and filling in the holes around sapling after sapling, most of which were now massive mature trees. The dogs of Coatshill had a lot to thank William Abernethy for if they only realised it.

On one such walk he was thinking seriously of upgrading to a more expensive and impressive set of darts for the Friday night darts tournaments when something caught his eye. At first he wasn't sure why, but he found himself standing and gazing at a white tabby cat sprawling in the sun on the front pathway of a garden he had been about to walk past. Perhaps he had developed a professional curiosity towards all cats he mused but this one had definitely caught his attention. It was very white but had one small black area at the very top of its left ear.

"Well what do you know?" he said to himself, "Snowy."

He slowly circled back to the front gate of the house as nonchalantly as possible but realised that it had a metal catch which looked rusty and might make a noise when opened. To the left of the property there was a driveway without any form of gate. He again made his way to it with as much stealth as possible and seeing that Snowy had not moved, proceeded up the paving slabs of the driveway in the direction of the front door. Just as he got to within six feet of the cat it looked round as if considering whether or not George constituted any form of threat. If Snowy came to any conclusion on that score he arrived at it too late. George covered the last few paces at a gallop and had Snowy by the scruff of her neck before she could run off. George tucked the screaming, scratching, meowing monster she had become into the front of his jacket and held her there. Although she was clearly doing her best to inflict pain on her attacker, with some success, George managed to hold on all the way back down the driveway and for the half mile or so of the journey home. Once inside his house he locked the door, pointed the front of his jacket at the cat carrier and let Snowy out. She bolted straight forward and into the cage which George locked immediately. He then slumped onto one of his kitchen chairs before examining the damage to his chest.

There were a number of scratch marks across his torso, most of which were quite shallow but there was one on his stomach where Snowy's claw must have caught his belly button that was much deeper and had been bleeding.

George's mother had been a stickler for dressing wounds and he had learned from her how to do it properly. He started by taking a shower and washing himself thoroughly even though the cuts stung like mad. Then he towelled himself, carefully avoiding any blood from the deepest of the cuts. This he dried with some toilet paper and then dabbed it with some disinfectant before finally putting on the largest plaster he could find.

Once he was sure that no further blood would be flowing, he got dressed in his a fresh dress shirt and tie, his suit and the better of his two pairs of black shoes. After a quick inspection he made himself a cup of tea and then sat down beside the phone. He savoured the taste of several sips of tea before picking up the handset and dialling the number from the first page of his notebook.

"Hello Ms Johnson," he said when the call was answered. "This is Milne, George Milne the Cat Detective. I have found Snowy for you."

Chapter Ten

Frankie had always been ambitious. Any opportunity to expand his franchise in the distribution of hard drugs had been jumped upon. Anyone who had stood in his way had submitted or strangely disappeared. With this ruthless approach to business he had become the leading drugs baron in Coatshill quite quickly. That provided a generous income and would have funded a lavish lifestyle if he had chosen to go down that route. Instead Frankie had continued to live a relatively modest lifestyle in the top floor tenement flat he shared with his sister Evelyn while squirreling away any cash that he could. In the days before political correctness, Evelyn had been described as a few pennies short of a shilling, two buns short of a picnic and by other similarly unkind expressions. Anyone who used such terms in front of Frankie immediately regretted it but there was no getting away from the fact that she struggled with day to day reality and Frankie's lifestyle in particular.

. . . .

Frankie looked down one day on his latest acquisition as it waddled about in the bath at number 10 Woodend Walk.

"It's no very big," said Willie McBride.

"Of course it's no very big," countered Frankie. "It's just a fucking baby. Wait till it's all grown up. Then it'll scare the shit out of everyone."

"What exactly is it," Asked Willie.

"It's a fucking Nile crocodile," said Frankie. "The worst man-eaters you can get."

Willie looked at young Rambo and thought he had some growing to do before he would compete in the scary leagues with him, but then mighty oaks and all that.

"He's cute though," added Willie without thinking things through.

"He's no fucking cute," said Frankie angrily, "He's a fucking man eater in the making. Just wait till we get him fed up a bit and full size. Then one look at him and folk'll wish it was just you snapping at their fingers and toes. I saw this documentary once about Mexican drug gangs and this guy in the medallion cartel had an alligator which he used to scare anyone who owed him money. Then he would cut them up and feed them to it. That was just an alligator. They're fannies compared to crocs, especially Nile crocs. I'll get him into the way of it by feeding him some fingers and toes till he's big enough to bite them off himself. That way he'll get a taste for people who owe me money."

Frankie smiled a typically emotionless smile but Willie didn't join in. It was partly due to an element of doubt as to Rambo's potential and partly due to offended professional pride.

Oblivious to all of the subtleties of the discussions above him, Rambo continued to splash about in Frankie's bath and snap occasionally at the bits of raw meat which had been placed on the half paving slab which now rested in the middle of the bath.

....

On one of Frankie's regular trips into Glasgow and in one of his favourite nightclubs he was approached by a very well dressed figure who introduced himself as Jim Simmons. Now Frankie had heard of Gentleman Jim Simmons who was one of the leading suppliers of hard drugs in the city but he had never set eyes on him before. As Jim sat down in the booth beside him there was a slight feeling of unease on Frankie's part which wasn't entirely neutralised by Willie McBride's presence beside him. Partly this was due to Jim's reputation and partly it was due to the massive thugs who sat down in the booth next door.

This pair, Frankie recognised as Ben and Jerry, two Polish bodybuilders that Jim employed as enforcers and personal body guards. Their names were not in fact Ben and Jerry. Admittedly, Jedrzej quite easily became Jerry when he moved to Scotland. Zbygniew's name defeated all the Scots who tried to pronounce it, and as he was an inch taller than Jerry,' Tom' was a non-starter. Thus for simplicity they became Ben and Jerry soon after they arrived and grew to quite like the names. At first they took any jobs going, in factories, on farms or wherever there was overtime as they built up savings for the eventual return to Poland. All the while they worked out in the nearest gym to their work place, piling on pounds of muscle as they went. Through this activity they were offered work on the doors of pubs or clubs, having first gained their SIA accreditation. It was on the door of one of Glasgow's roughest city centre pubs that they came to the attention of Gentleman Jim Simmons. A conversation and a drink after work one evening resulted in them gaining well paid employment on his staff, initially as his personal bodyguards whenever he had to move around town. It was a small step from there to debt collecting from anyone careless enough to have outstanding debts due to Jim. If Ben and Jerry showed up at your doorway you would immediately pay anything you owed. Even if you didn't owe Jim anything you would probably want to pay up anyway.

Their reputation as effective enforcers grew without them having to inflict violence on a regular basis, a state of affairs which suited them both. They had arrived in Scotland to make their fortune after all, not to become gangsters. On occasions though, they would have no option but to resort to violence. When this did happen, it was usually housekeeping within their own industry involving either a rival drug-dealer or a wavering team member. In these circumstances, they would always really go to town.

"You must be Francis Cook," oozed Jim Simmons in a beautifully smooth manner. "I've heard a lot about you from my friends in Lanarkshire. I'm glad we are getting a chance to meet. Can I get you a drink?"

Frankie considered his usual vodka and blackcurrant and decided it might be inappropriate in present company. He reckoned he could talk as posh as anyone else and put on his version of well-spoken to appear on level terms with Jim. He regularly attempted to level the playing field in this way when talking to the big fish in his industry. As a result his speech often veered from the vernacular to BBC English on an almost random basis.

"If you're paying let's have Champers." He said with his customary bravado.

"Excellent choice," agreed Jim, "and as this is my establishment I insist on paying."

"I didn't realise this was your place," said Frankie, genuinely impressed.

"It wasn't until last week," said Jim. "Squaring of debts and all that."

Now Frankie was worried but refused to let it show. Willie sat next to him giving it his best shot to do likewise while not being too intimidated by the large gents sitting in the neighbouring booth, both of whom were sizing him up in a very professional manner.

A passing waitress took Jim's order with a forced smile and the men sat staring at each other for a few minutes before Jim spoke.

"As I say, I've heard a lot about you from my friends in Lanarkshire. Good things. I'm impressed at the way you run your business in Coatshill. You have a very similar approach to discipline to myself, although I don't share your fascination with fingers and toes. However you run a tight ship as it were and I admire that."

Frankie made a point of staring at Jim without blinking, wondering where on earth this conversation was going.

"I have extended my business interests into Lanarkshire recently as I'm sure you know," Jim continued. "It has proved to be a profitable move but has not come about without effort on my part and has taken up a lot of my staff's time. This has put some pressure on my Glasgow operations. Long story short, Francis, it is difficult to find good staff. I appreciate you have always been your own man as it were and I respect that; however, I would like you to consider an expansion of your interests through what we could call a franchise arrangement."

Jim Simmons paused for a second to gauge the effect of his conversation so far.

"I'm listening," said Frankie who hated being called Francis but felt obliged to let it pass on this occasion.

"Good man," continued Jim. "My thinking is along the lines of you keeping your existing operations in Coatshill but taking over the day to day running of all my interests in Lanarkshire. For a price, you would get to keep 50% of the profits. I would leave the management arrangements to you but you would buy only from me. In addition to your own support staff…" At this point he looked at Willie with a less than complimentary look. "You would have my word on the street behind you, and if necessary additional staff available in a crisis."

With this he looked over at the two large gentlemen in the neighbouring booth who had now stopped staring at Willie and were eyeing up the talent on the dance floor instead.

Frankie's mind was working furiously, assimilating the possibilities on offer. This was a chance to join the big time. He had been able to put almost £2million away in cash over the last 10 years but that was loose change compared to the scale of Jim Simmons' turnover. There was also the probability that Jim was making Frankie an offer he couldn't refuse in every sense. But it was also a huge pat on the back to have Jim make this offer. Frankie knew he had arrived.

"I'm very interested," he managed to say after a minute's pause. "You said for a price. What is your price for this... franchise?"

Jim smiled, "Good boy, straight to the heart of the matter. I have decided to invest in a rather large property abroad and as a result I need an equally large sum of money. The price for Lanarkshire is £3 million in cash."

Jim watched closely for Frankie's reaction. It appeared to be cool enough.

Frankie knew this was unlikely to be a negotiable figure. He also knew that he didn't have that amount in readies. He could possibly get the additional £1 million in a few months of running the whole hard drugs set-up for Lanarkshire but it would take him years if he had to rely on Coatshill alone.

"That figure seems appropriate," he said calmly. "However, I need to be sure that the arrangement stacks up. No offence."

"Not at all old boy," said Jim. "What were your thoughts around that area?"

"Well," started Frankie, making his pitch. "I am happy enough to cough up £1.5million up front but the balance would be payable after say... six months when things have proved their worth."

"I see where you are coming from," countered Jim talking as if he were discussing the sale of a legitimate business, as ever. "I really see £2 million up front and the rest after three months as a more realistic option."

Frankie stared back without blinking, "let's compromise then. £1.5 million up front, but the balance after three months."

Jim stared back without a hint of a blink. "Can you deliver that, my friend?" he asked.

"Oh yes," replied Frankie immediately, ignoring any doubts he might have had in the back of his mind regarding the slight gap in his finances. He reckoned he could make it up one way or another within the three months or stall if necessary. Either way he had reached the big time and there was no looking back.

"Let's shake on that," said Jim as the champagne finally arrived. "I work on the basis that people I work with deliver what they promise or suffer accordingly."

"I deliver," said Frankie.

The waitress opened the bottle of champagne with an element of practiced skill and filled two glasses. She looked round to indicate a question as to whether Willie and his two new colleagues were included in the round and quickly ascertained from the look on both Jim and Frankie's faces that they were not.

"Here's to a very profitable business arrangement," toasted Jim.

"Let's make money," toasted Frankie in return.

Chapter Eleven

Gentleman Jim Simmons was a self-made criminal millionaire several times over and had run the bulk of the drugs trade in central Glasgow's nightclubs for almost ten years. Unlike many of his rivals he had started out in life with many advantages, growing up in a comfortable middle class home in Giffnock with two parents who both worked and two siblings to argue and fight with in the safety of a loving home. He seemed destined to follow in his parents' footsteps as he made steady progress through his primary and secondary schools. An intelligent boy with a quick wit and reasonable sporting talents, he was also popular with his class mates. The girls in his class found him not unattractive and he had a number of girlfriends in his teenage years. By the time he was ready to leave school he had a good collection of qualifications and had gained a place at Strathclyde University to study Computer Science. He was also a reasonable rugby player on the wing and was an accomplished sailor, having taken up the sport on nearby Lochwinnoch.

After a care free summer partying with his friends and a holiday in Greece he headed off to University ready to take the world by storm. A fun-packed Freshers' week was followed by a gentle introduction to the Computer Science Department and the Maths department and their staffs. Cheese and wine flowed and Jim felt at home.

Slowly but surely, though, as the classes and tutorials started in earnest he realised that not only did he have no interest in the subjects that he had chosen, but also that the mathematics side of the course was way beyond his abilities. As he struggled more and more he attended less and less till finally he stopped going to any of the formal parts of his course.

To fill his day he instead became a regular attender of both the University gym and the Students' Union. After a healthy hour or two in the gym he would head for the pool room and play until he felt hungry. Then he would treat himself to lunch in the canteen followed by copious quantities of beer in one of the student bars. There he would dull his guilt at abandoning his studies with other like-minded individuals. He became very strong in a bulky sort of way, very good at pool and something of a mystery to the course lecturers.

Eventually a day of reckoning came and after a brief meeting with his tutor, who had largely been unable to put a face to the name beforehand, he was kicked out shortly after Easter.

Undeterred and with some money he had managed to put aside from playing pool for money, he headed off to travel Europe, sending his distraught parents a postcard with an abridged version of events to date. Over the next few years he gained experience as a barman, waiter, bouncer and, briefly, as a gigolo to a lonely Italian trophy wife. He grew in worldly experience, physical bulk and in the number of contacts he had around Europe where a free bed for the night might be found.

It was while working in Berlin that he first got involved in the drugs trade. One evening, while he was working in a less than fashionable bar, a Russian gangster came in looking for Jim's boss. Jim answered honestly, that he hadn't seen him for a few days and that the chef, who'd worked there for years, had been opening up and closing the place with his set of keys. Without another word the Russian walked behind the bar and through to the kitchen. He returned after ten minutes or so, thanked Jim and left.

A few minutes passed before a very shaken French chef appeared from the kitchen.

"What was all that about?" Jim asked him.

"Looks like we will both need a new job soon, mon ami . Stefan owes that guy a lot of money and needs to pay up today. I had to tell him where Stefan is hiding. I had no choice."

Jim nodded, fully understanding the nature of the recent discussion which had taken place in the kitchen.

Still shaking the Frenchman removed his chef's apron and threw it and the keys down on the counter.

"If you do see Stefan again, tell him I quit. Good luck."

With that he left the bar and Jim never saw him again. He also never saw Stefan again and, armed with the keys of the bar, started running it as his own. At first he ran it in a way it could be handed back to Stefan should he reappear, but as time went by Jim treated it as his very own business. He had already helped with orders and stock-taking, so it was a small step to doing all the paperwork. Jim had no intention of being there forever but he realised that if he could keep things ticking over long enough he could leave with a pocket full of cash and an office full of unpaid bills in Stefan's name.

After a few month of this arrangement he was taken aback one night to see the same Russian gangster enter the bar. The Russian was surprised to see Jim still there but nodded and smiled a fairly thin smile. Jim nodded back, trying to look as calm as he could.

"Would you like a drink?" he asked the Russian.

"Vodka and ice," came the reply. "I was passing and was curious to see who was running the bar now. I am surprised you stayed after… " His voice trailed off in a way that suggested Stefan had not been breathing for some time now.

"I thought I would stay on till Stefan returned or it was taken over. I like Berlin."

The Russian stared at Jim and was impressed at the calm stare which he saw in return.

"Maybe I'm the new owner," the Russian continued.

"Maybe you are."

"Would the books balance, or would I discover a bundle of cash missing and a single employee with his bags packed?"

Jim considered a number of options. He was as big as the Russian was and a good bit stronger. As long as the Russian didn't pull a gun or a knife Jim reckoned he could win a scrap if necessary then leg it before help arrived. There was something else though which had arisen in Jim. It was an admiration of the way this guy moved and spoke which stemmed from a deep rooted confidence. He was a gangster, had no doubt killed people and didn't seem to care who knew it. Jim found this fascinating and frightening at the same time.

"You'd discover a bundle of cash missing but no bags. Like I said, I like Berlin."

There was a tense pause before the Russian burst out laughing. "I like you English. You have balls. I am Grigori." With that the Russian put out his hand and Jim shook it.

There followed an evening which changed the course of Jim's life for ever. He had grown up with hopes of being rich and successful but his early failure at University had put that on hold till now. Grigori was heavily involved in the distribution of hard drugs in Berlin and was a regular enforcer for a number of Russian suppliers around Germany. He liked his work and it made him a very good living. He "took shit from nobody" as he put it but was always on the lookout for new opportunities and any like-minded individuals to do business with. Stefan had had an expensive cocaine habit and was way behind with the cost of it. With his brains fried he had refused an offer he couldn't refuse from Grigori and his associates which involved using the bar as a hub for some of their drug dealing but also a lot of their money laundering. Nobody turned down their offers and got away with it so Stefan had disappeared one night. The very night, in fact that Grigori had first spoken to Jim.

The idea of using the bar was still very much alive but required someone to run it on a day to day basis. Jim appeared to fit the bill and also didn't seem fazed by whatever else was required to make a success of the venture. The two men talked for hours, slowly relaxing in each other's company through a combination of growing mutual respect and increasing blood alcohol levels. At midnight Grigori suggested the bar should be closed and that they should hit the town together. At this suggestion the remaining two customers drank up and left without further encouragement and Jim and Grigori, by now well-oiled and up for anything, hit the town.

The night was a wild one of drinking and fighting and ended up in a brothel which Grigori seemed to know well and may even have owned. Jim kept pace with his new friend in all things. Drinking certainly, picking and winning fights with soldiers also, and finally in still being able to bed one of the ladies of very easy virtue in the very early hours of the next day.

A firm friendship was born that night and during the course of all the activities he agreed to stay and run the Blue Max bar for Grigori. It was further agreed that he would keep all the money he had pocketed so far, which in all honesty was very small change, and would keep any profits from the sale of drink or food. In addition he would use the bar as a selling place for drugs, none of which would actually be kept on the premises, and he would also accept payments from

Grigori's customers who would, thereafter, regularly stop by and pay up.

This arrangement grew and developed over the next few years as Grigori and his business partners expanded their empire in and around Berlin. Jim became very wealthy from his increasing share of their activities. The two friends would hold regular business meetings on a sailing boat which Jim bought and kept on nearby Lake Tegel. Here, away from any prying eyes they would discuss business, drink and plan for the future. Sometimes they would bring along some of the girls from Grigori's brothels and Jim would treat them to a display of his sailing prowess. Afterwards they would regularly have wild parties in down town Berlin, paying little attention to the law or the upholders of the law, safe in their world of extreme wealth.

After five years or so he managed to return to Glasgow for a holiday and made peace with his parents and his siblings. He was vague with the details of his businesses in Berlin, referring to them only as entertainment and the family didn't push for more detail. His parents were just happy to see their son again, healthy, happy and obviously prospering. His brother and sister were happy to see him again too, even before he bought each of them a new car. He hinted with them about some of the wilder sides of Berlin nightlife but missed out any direct mention of criminality. He spent a happy and relaxing ten days at his parents' house before returning once more to the daily grind of his life in Berlin. After all, in his line of work it didn't pay to be away for too long. You never knew who might take over in his absence, even with Grigori minding the store.

On his return, though, he found it difficult to settle down again. Something about his stay in Glasgow had left its mark. Maybe it was spending time with his family or perhaps seeing the old familiar places from his childhood again. Either way, something had moved him deep inside and he was keen to go back on a more permanent basis.

Jim's business interests in Berlin were very lucrative and not the type of business concerns which could be easily relocated. If he was going to relocate to Glasgow it would need to be handled carefully. He had a large amount of money spirited away and a fair proportion of it laundered and more easily transferrable as legitimate funds. His main concern, however, was what his business partners would think. He would have to tread warily with that one.

One evening, when he was having a late night drinking session with Grigori, he decided to raise the subject.

"I looked around Glasgow when I was back there and saw a lot of money to be made."

"Are you homesick, my friend?" asked Grigori immediately.

"Aren't we all, but there is a huge industry there with vast profits to be made none the less."

Grigori looked at his friend and smiled.

"I am homesick too, but I am not able to return to Russia for a number of reasons so I have made my home here. It is not a bad life we lead," as he waved a hand round the brothel where they sat, indicating the young women sitting at tables nearby.

"But if you could go home to Russia and set up a business there which was as profitable as the ones you have here, would you? That is my point."

Grigori's face fell as he obviously considered what that would be like for him.

"I do not have that option, my friend," he said sadly. "But you do, it is true. Let us look into it together, but you must be able to prove to me that the business case stacks up. For example, who runs the trade there at the moment? Who are the bigger fish who supply them? Are you looking at a joint venture or a straight takeover? There is much to be considered."

"I have given this some thought already," said Jim.

"I thought that might be the case," added Grigori calmly.

"At a local level from Bargeddie, through Garthamlock and Maryhill to Old Kilpatrick the distribution is controlled by gangs who've lived there all their lives and know their patches inside out. It isn't feasible to takeover those operations. But at a higher level if we took over the supply chain going into Glasgow and cut the prices, at least initially, we could bring a lot of the locals on-board. Those that play ball get our support with imported muscle on call. Those that don't will fall by the wayside and their territories will become available for the expansion of our people."

"I don't know these cities you speak of but perhaps we can do this and you can go home," said Grigori getting unsteadily to his feet. "For now though, I am going to get laid and so are you, my friend."

They stuck to both plans, getting laid that night (not a difficult thing to achieve in a brothel you own) and in the following months, making the necessary plans for Jim to return to Glasgow on a permanent and professional basis, something which proved far more difficult to achieve.

Jim did however return and he started to cultivate as many contacts and associates in the Glasgow drug dealing fraternity as he could. This was a potentially dangerous business, as a dozen petty squabbles existed there at any moment in time. Slowly though, he became a known face on the scene without anybody really knowing what his role was. Once he had gained enough information to know who was who and to judge who would be the best long term business partners, his plan with Grigori swung swiftly into action.

Firstly two car bombs in Spain removed two of the main suppliers of drugs to the UK. Then a number of targeted shootings in Glasgow thinned out the number of conflicts and swung them in favour of Jim and Grigori's chosen future business associates. As the supply of hard drugs from the Spanish connection dried up Jim let it be known that he could fill the shortages at particularly attractive prices. Within a remarkably short period of time he was supplying 60% of Glasgow's drug gangs with Grigori's sourced drugs. He bought and then ring-fenced a number of fashionable city centre pubs and clubs and personally controlled the hugely profitable white collar drug trade there. There were a few objections to the new regime, especially as the prices went up, but Jim had sufficient out of town muscle to silence any dissenters without anybody being able to point the finger with any degree of accuracy.

Soon after the plan began, Jim and Grigori had established themselves as the main players in town.

The money flowed in and soon the main problem was what to do with it all. Jim diversified into some of the neighbouring areas such as Lanarkshire and Ayrshire but soon found that he was spreading his operations too thin for them to be policed properly. A business meeting with Grigori followed and it was decided to franchise out some of the outlying areas to potential partners to consolidate the international supply without stretching the local manpower at Jim's disposal. This tactic had served Grigori and his associates well over the years and he saw no reason to believe it wouldn't do so again in the West of Scotland. Jim started to put feelers out to see who was the best candidate to do business with in each area, and who could put up the necessary starting funds to buy their way in. After all, they weren't running a charity.

Chapter Twelve

With the safe return of Snowy, George's reputation spread like wildfire throughout the mature, cat-owning ladies of Coatshill and indeed wider Lanarkshire. It could not have been described as a flood, but there was, however, a steady stream of phone calls to George's mobile from distressed ladies whose cats had gone astray.

George established a pattern to his response. He felt it unfair to make overambitious promises which he might not be able to fulfil. As a result he always emphasised a huge existing workload, real or imagined. He promised only to try and fit in their case where possible. All this for a reduced fee of £100 each time, with the balance of a further £100 if and when he found their cat. He discovered, however, that money was rarely an issue with these desperate women - with only one exception they were always women - and most insisted on paying his full fee up front. He had no great hope of finding any of the cats but he provided some element of hope. Indeed he was merely selling hope at a reasonable price.

To increase the value of the hope he was selling, he had some business cards printed with his name in bold print and the words 'Cat Detective' underneath. He noticed the effect these had on his clients whenever he handed one to them. They would read it and relax perceptibly: Now there was a professional on the case. As a result he put his prices up. Even to take on a case, clients had to pay £150 up front and a further £150 on delivery of the missing beast. He managed to stop himself saying dead or alive each time, but only just.

Over the next few months he built up a sizeable client base of owners pining for missing cats. Although he never personally found any more of them, some cases resolved themselves as a few returned to their owners homes after a sabbatical. At least two were found dead on roads near the homes of their owners and on such occasions George would manage to sound suitably sympathetic on hearing the news.

Initially when he had left the employment of Coatshill District Council, George had vaguely thought that he may have to seek part time employment in the future. At the time, he had no real notion of what type of work that might be. As the cat-searching business had largely been delivered on a plate to his door, long before any need to augment his savings, George had decided not to look this particular gift horse in the mouth. At the level of business he was taking on, after six months or so he calculated that he could pay his bills without eating into his savings at all. If this kept up he could maybe even make it to retirement without genuinely working ever again.

Chapter Thirteen

Gentleman Jim Simmons got out of his Range Rover and looked with distaste at number 10 Woodend Walk. He lived in a large property in Bearsden which was surrounded by an extensive and well-tended garden. He preferred to spend his time there where high fences and security cameras ensured his safety. When he did leave it was usually for a quick visit to one of his front businesses or for an exotic holiday somewhere warm and sunny. To leave his lovely home to visit Lanarkshire was bad enough but to have to visit a top floor tenement flat in Coatshill was as bad as it got. His minders took up their positions in front of him and behind while his driver kept a close watch on the rest of the street.

Jim climbed the stairs at a steady pace until his group reached the top. There they found a heavy steel door opened for them and Frankie standing there with a welcoming smile.

"Welcome to my humble home," he said amiably.

"As fucking humble as they get," thought Jim to himself.

"Bijou, Francis," he said to Frankie who had no idea what that meant. "Very secure though, I expect," he added with professional approval.

The two men entered the flat and made their way to the front room. For once it did not contain Evelyn engrossed in daytime television. Frankie had taken the precaution of packing her off to the hairdressers with a carer, to ensure he and Jim could discuss business without interruptions.

As Jim entered he looked round and noticed a strange figure standing near the curtains beside two enormous suitcases. The figure was of average height and build. His face had a number of old scars and both sets of knuckles had tattoos, both of which read 'hate'. He was expressionless, showing neither welcome nor hostility towards Frankie's visitors.

"Spider here has been guarding the money," said Frankie.

"I see," said Jim who noticed that despite the size difference, his two minders were eyeing Spider with caution. He sat down as indicated and politely refused the offer of anything to eat or drink.

"Sorry to rush things, but probably best for both of us to spend as little time as possible in the same location. Security and all that. I assume you have the down payment in those suitcases."

Frankie nodded as coolly as he could.

Jim then took a mobile phone from one of his pockets and a matchbox from another.

"This phone is unused and completely off the radar of Police Scotland. In the matchbox is a SIM card with 198 contacts who will phone you from now on with their requirements. There is a number marked 'Universal exports' for you to place the orders with my associates. You will receive a text with an order number, a collection point, price and time where they can be uplifted. Thereafter the distribution and collection of payment falls to you and your organisation."

Jim looked straight at Frankie. "Okay so far?"

"Simples," replied Frankie with a smile.

"Once you have each complete payment, you will text the same phone number with the order number and wait for a time and place to drop off the cash, keeping 15% of all amounts as your share of the business. Every payment has to be made within two weeks of collection of the goods. Clear?"

Frankie nodded again.

"I do not permit any late payments at any level of my business. Clear?"

Frankie nodded again.

"It goes without saying that the information stored on this SIM card must not fall into anyone else's hands and especially not the police. I would regard that as… unforgiveable carelessness."

He stared at Frankie who stared back without blinking and nodded his understanding. Then Frankie turned and nodded to Spider who, moving for the first time, carried the suitcases to the other side of the room and placed them in front of Ben and Jerry. Then he returned to his place beside the curtains and folded his arms, his duty completed.

Ben and Jerry opened the suitcases briefly to make sure they were full of cash then closed them tightly without counting it.

Business concluded, Jim stood up and grasped Frankie's hand in a tight handshake. Frankie stood up too and again offered Jim tea, coffee or something stronger to seal the deal.

"No thank you, Francis, I have some cash to transfer."

"Don't you want to check it?" asked Frankie.

"No need, old boy. I trust you have it all there."

"Okay then," said Frankie slightly deflated at Jim's haste. "Let me show you something before you go though. You'll love this."

Frankie indicated the direction of his bathroom and Jim followed him reluctantly. Ben and Jerry eyed the situation with caution but noticed that neither Spider nor Willie McBride had moved and were clearly not expecting any trouble. Jim noticed this too and shrugged his shoulders in their direction as if to say let me indulge him. Jim edged into the bathroom after Frankie and stared with curiosity at Rambo.

"A pet crocodile?" he asked.

"For now," replied Frankie. "He'll soon fill out and scare the shit out of anyone who owes us money. Bill the butcher is keeping him well fed."

"Is he one of your enforcers?"

"No," said Frankie confused. "He's my fucking butcher."

"I see," said Jim. "Whatever it takes, Francis old boy. Whatever it takes."

Jim headed out of the bathroom and collected Ben and Jerry. He shook Frankie's hand, again emphasising timeous payments all round were the key, and headed out and down the stairs. As the three men walked out of the close and headed back to the Range Rover Jim looked back at the tenement. As he did so he noticed an elderly man with a bald head looking out of the right hand side, ground floor flat. There was something familiar about him, Jim thought to himself. As he got into the vehicle he suddenly realised who he had seen.

"Well, well you old rascal, so that's where you've been hiding is it," and he chuckled to himself.

Chapter Fourteen

The police raid on Frankie's flat had been planned in great detail. For the event itself all police leave had been cancelled in Coatshill. Additional personnel had been drafted in from Glasgow for the operation, including specialist firearms officers. The details of what was happening were known only to a few of the officers involved. Jimmy Bell was chosen to lead the entry team as the whole thing was his idea and he decided who got to do what. The planning was helped by a mountain of intelligence gained over three months by a major undercover operation. The main plank of this was the use of the ground floor flat on the left hand side of number 10 Woodend Walk.

Two police officers, one male and one female had posed as a newly married couple, Mr and Mrs Caldwell, renting the property and had moved in with all the usual requirements to set up a first home. Such great care had been taken in selecting a credible couple that the two had hit it off immediately to such an extent that they had consummated their surveillance duties after only three days during a breathless changeover of shifts. Despite this happy occurrence they managed to stay focussed on the task at hand and produced detailed reports of everyone who came and went from the top floor flats, including poor Miss Blackery, who was only discounted as an accomplice after thorough checks had been carried out on her background. She would have been horrified to learn about all the different agencies who were asked to vouch for her and outraged if she thought for a second that the nice young couple on the ground floor ("so much in love") had had anything to do with it.

It took less time to ascertain if old Mr Wilson was on Santa's naughty or nice list. A couple of enquiries showed that he was a lifelong villain with a poor ability to avoid imprisonment. He had a criminal record like few others and had associated both inside prison and outside with many of Frankie Cook's closest members of staff. That led to further investigations and after a night-time recce by that nice Mr Caldwell from the ground floor flat, a thin wire was discovered running from Baldy Wilson's rear window to the rear window of Frankie's top floor flat. Cutting this at an appropriate moment was built into the planning for Jimmy Bell's raid, as it had come to be called.

When Mr and Mrs Caldwell reported a visit by Jim Simmons of Glasgow to Frankie's flat, at the end of which his sidekicks were seen to leave with two bulging suitcases, the date of the raid was immediately brought forward, with a close watch kept to ensure nothing of note left the flat in between.

At the appointed hour one of the team cut the wire from Baldy's flat and signalled control that the early warning system had been neutralised. The entry team then rushed from two unmarked vans parked along the street from number 10 and ran headlong up the stairs. At the top, out of breath but fortified by adrenalin, they started to batter against the steel door whilst shouting, "Police. Open up!"

Frankie was initially taken by surprise by the lack of warning but recovered quickly enough to put into place the necessary measures to survive the raid. As no drugs or money were on the premises this was limited to hiding the SIM cards from his phones. A range of options for this had been identified and rehearsed many times. Evelyn's black cat was sitting peacefully on her lap on the sofa when the noise at the door started. Evelyn managed to calm the cat down long enough for Frankie to grab it roughly by the neck and hold it down while Willie took the SIM cards out of both business phones and then placed them inside the small barrel attached to Raven's collar. Once that was secured the cat was released and it screeched and bolted for the hall cupboard.

The second part of Frankie's early warning system was the strength of the steel door and the concrete and steel surround which had been constructed around it. It took the police team five minutes to fail to open it. Inside Frankie had time to make a fresh cup of tea and once settled back on his chair indicated to Willie to open the door. Willie timed it perfectly to coincide with the team's regular collisions with the door and three burly policemen and an equally burly policewoman tumbled through the suddenly open gap and collapsed in a heap on Frankie's hall carpet.

"Do come in," Willie managed to say, before being rugby-tackled by three policemen rushing past the prostrated entry group. They floored him and cuffed him while another group rushed past and into the front room where they found Frankie sitting calmly with a cup of tea in one hand and a half eaten digestive biscuit in the other.

"Is there a problem, officer?" he asked a sweating and angry Jimmy Bell who signalled the other officers in his group to cuff Frankie anyway.

"I have a search warrant," he shouted waving it in front of Frankie's face.

"You fucking better have," came the reply as Frankie was sat on and cuffed. "And a joiner to fix my door."

"Take him away and search every fucking orifice," Jimmy shouted at his colleagues who were enjoying all this excitement. Jimmy looked round the flat and saw Evelyn sitting quietly on the sofa still watching the news.

By then the entry team had got to their feet and rushed to support their colleagues in the front room, hoping to meet more resistance on the way. The burly female officer came through into the front room and Jimmy ordered her to take Evelyn to the station and search her thoroughly. He looked at Evelyn's frightened stare as the policewoman helped her to her feet and reached for a set of handcuffs.

"You won't need these," he instructed before adding. "Take it easy with her too. But search her thoroughly."

There then followed a thorough search of the flat by the specialists from Coatshill and their colleagues from Glasgow. A moment of light relief occurred at the start of this process when WPC Johnston began searching the hall cupboard and was scratched and bitten by a now traumatised Raven. She made a second grab for it but was too slow and Raven ran straight out the front door and down the stairs before anyone could stop her. The next 20 minutes were passed with various comments being made about WPC Johnston's pussy. Some funny; most not. It only stopped when Jimmy told them to shut up and concentrate on the job in hand. He was starting to have the uneasy feeling that they were not going to find anything they could pin on Frankie. That is, apart of course, from keeping a dangerous animal without the necessary licence. Rambo had been discovered early on but there was a shortage of volunteers to remove him for further examination and so an expert had to be called from Edinburgh Zoo's Reptile House. Over the next few days he was tasked with examining the animal and any excretions to see if it hid any of Frankie's secrets. Sadly for Jimmy, just like Frankie's flat, it did not.

Chapter Fifteen

"How the fuck do you find a cat?" asked Frankie to nobody in particular.

The regulars in The Ranch had been listening to his many complaints that night in a polite state of fear. Frankie was not his happy, calm, usual self tonight in his local. Something was playing on his mind and had him worried and irritable which in turn made his audience worried and fearful. It appeared that his sister's cat had run off and for whatever reason Frankie was desperate to get it back.

"Why don't you ask our very own Cat Detective to find it?" said Old Jock.

Frankie looked at him to see if he was taking the piss, an error which might have cost Jock his life from the look on Frankie's face. It was clear however that Jock was quite serious.

"What are you blethering about?" Frankie asked.

"There's a guy drinks in here who's a Cat Detective. George Milne, the Cat detective." As Jock said it, he looked round for corroboration from the others in the bar but discovered that they were all looking away or examining their beers with sudden intense interest.

"Well, he's found a few cats, but it's a scam really. He gets money off old ladies whose cats are missing, telling them he will try to find them. That's all. But it's a con, Frankie," said Willie Taylor.

"But he's found some cats for folk?" asked Frankie.

"Oh aye, he's found loads," persisted Jock, ignoring the looks from the others to shut up.

Jock was staring at Willie Taylor who was trying to do a cutting action across his throat without Frankie seeing it.

"He is a fucking Cat Detective," Jock continued, as unstoppable as ever. "That's what you bastards call him isn't it? The Cat Detective. What's the matter? I'm just saying…" But as ever he was just saying far too much

"Where does he live?" said Frankie. "I've a wee job for him and he better not try any scam with me."

The others had given up and left Jock to lead death and destruction to George Milne's door by giving away his address and very detailed directions of how to get there to Wacky Frank Cook.

Chapter Sixteen

George Milne sat in his favourite chair with a fresh mug of coffee beside him on the wine table. His feet were up, on a padded foot rest which he had bought for his mother and was exactly the right height to provide comfortable support. His feet were in pair of broken-in, fleece-lined slippers from Marks and Spencer which kept his feet lovely and warm whatever the time of year. The television was on showing the BBC news channel and he was enjoying the second of three chocolate digestive biscuits he had brought with the coffee from the kitchen. He had no work to do. He had no requirement to go anywhere that day if he chose not to. Online banking had confirmed that yet again, this month his cat-searching business had brought in enough to cover all of his modest bills. Indeed, it had been such a good month for him and such a bad month for cats that he would be able to transfer £125 to his ISA account. To put the icing on the cake he had received an envelope from National Savings and Investments that morning to inform him that ERNIE had decided he should win £25 from that month's Premium Bond Prize Draw.

All in all life was good for George. His decision to leave the council had been vindicated by his good fortune since and he was now enjoying the fruits of success. Nothing, he mused, could spoil the comfortable life he had created for himself. It may not be exciting but it was safe and he could quietly enjoy the freedom it brought.

At that moment, Frankie Cook arrived at George's door and rang the bell.

"Who could that be?" George wondered to himself. He certainly wasn't expecting anyone. Maybe it was the postman with another letter from ERNIE which had got separated from the other good news in his sack. With a sigh George got up and answered the door.

When he opened it there was a rough looking man he had never seen before in his life standing on the front step. Before he could say anything Frankie got in first.

"Are you the Cat Detective?" he asked.

"Yes," said George with some hesitancy. Frankie did not have the look of a little old lady who doted on her precious pet cat.

"Good!" said Frankie pushing past George without an invite. "I need to talk to you."

George was worried as he followed this intruder into the front room of his own house. His first thought was that Frankie was related to one of his clients and had taken exception to George ripping them off. He resolved to repay anything owed to his aunt or mother or whoever it was without question.

"How can I help?" he asked noticing that Frankie had sat down in his favourite chair.

"I need you to find a cat and I need you to find it quickly," said Frankie.

George was both relieved and concerned at the same time.

"Is it your own cat that is missing?" he asked.

"No, it's ma sister's cat that's missing. She is very upset and I want you to find it and bring it back pronto."

"I'm afraid I'm really quite busy at this exact moment in time. I'm not sure I could take on any other business right now."

"No problem," said Frankie. "I'm sure you will take on this little bit of business and not even think about any other cat till you find Raven and that is non-negotiable. Clear?"

"Crystal," replied George as his shoulders sagged and he sat down on the sofa. He had managed to grab the notebook from his wine table as he did so and thought he better sound as professional as possible. "Can you give me a description of the missing cat please?"

"It's black and it's missing. What else do you need?"

"Where does your sister live?"

"She lives with me."

"More specifically…?"

"10 Woodend Walk. Do you know it?"

George nodded before continuing as calmly as he could. "Male or female?"

"I don't know. Does it matter?"

"It makes a big difference to the size, the habits, the likely behaviour etc. It really is quite important if I'm to find it."

"I don't know. I think it's female but you'd have to ask ma sister aw that."

"Name?" asked George with his pencilled poised in a professional way over the notebook.

"Evelyn."

George pondered for a second without written anything down, not entirely sure whose name he had just been given. "The cat's name?" he ventured not sure what would happen next.

"Raven," said Frankie as George breathed a sigh of relief. "Look, you better come round and ask Evelyn all of this shit. She'll be able to give you all the answers."

"Can you give me the phone number please?"

Frankie gave George the landline number of the flat, which was virtually never used, before adding, "I mean: find this cat quickly, like. Phone the morrow and get started the day."

With that Frankie stood up, swiped the last biscuit from the wine table and made his way swiftly to and through George's front door.

George had managed to stand up but did not feel inclined to follow Frankie. He heard the front door slam shut and collapsed again onto the sofa, feeling that for the moment at least his favourite chair was somehow tainted.

"Bugger!" he said out loud. So much for a peaceful and quiet life.

Chapter Seventeen

Janine seemed to be in a very chatty mood that Friday night but only, for some reason, with George. He was initially flattered and then quickly suspicious, as women rarely paid him much attention, especially women as attractive as Janine. Overall though, he was enjoying the attention. Attention which was not lost on his fellow dart players.

Willie Taylor started gently poking fun at George. "It's your turn if you can manage to tear yourself away from the bar staff."

It continued as the night wore on with the others joining in. Even old Jock felt bold enough to have a shot at George.

Truth be told, George didn't mind one little bit. Janine asked him about his health, his house, his predictions for the weather, his latest cat-detecting escapades and even if he ever saw Glenda these days? George answered quietly and honestly each time and allowed himself to stare more openly at Janine's figure as she became more interested in his life and as the beers took their inevitable effect.

As the night wore on the mood became friendlier and George felt he was part of a close group of friends in a way that he had rarely felt before. There was also the strange experience of a woman taking an interest in him for himself in a way that had never happened before. All was going swimmingly until Janine asked the question shortly before closing time: "Do you know Frankie Cook?"

It was as if the world had stopped revolving, the piano player in the western bar had stopped playing and the audience at a Jeremy Kyle show had all stopped and stared at George at the same moment in time.

"Why do you ask?" he managed to respond to Janine, more calmly than he could have predicted.

"Oh, no reason really," Janine lied in a voice that betrayed emotion for the first time that night.

"I have met the man and he has asked me to find his sister's cat," George replied in all honesty.

"Can we have a quiet word," asked Janine having judged that the remaining darts players were no longer interested in either George's ability at the ochie or her interest in George.

"Sure," said George, very unsure of where this conversation was going.

Janine ushered George towards one of the corner booths near the kitchen door and sat down beside him. She stared at him as if she were weighing up his ability to stand by her against the devil himself, which in a way she was.

"You know my daughter Rosie?" she asked.

"No," George answered quite honestly.

"Of course you do, she works here every Saturday night when I have a day off," persisted Janine.

"I only come in here to play darts on a Friday and a Sunday," countered George.

"Really! So you have never met my daughter Rosie? Never! Ever!" continued Janine.

"Honestly no!" Said George. "What does she look like?"

"If you had ever seen her and you are not gay, you would have remembered the encounter."

"I'm not gay," George confirmed defensively. "But I don't think I've met her."

"Okay," said Janine. "In that case I need a huge favour from you, because at the moment you are the only person I believe I can trust."

"Of course you can trust me," said George with no idea what was going on but drunk in the company of an intoxicating woman and drunk from seven pints of real ale.

"Frankie fucking Cook is convinced that Rosie is the girl of his dreams. Unfortunately for him she is not and is besotted with her girlfriend Carol, which creates something of a problem. Frankie has given her an ultimatum that she has to go on a date with him this weekend or he will do her in. If you know him at all you know he is capable of backing up his threats with extreme violence."

Janine was gushing now and was desperate for help in protecting her only daughter in a way that George was unfamiliar with but found quite addictive in his current state. She continued with descriptions of Frankie's exploits and her daughter's gentleness and innocence in comparison.

George was won over and was helpless in his support second only to the need to empty his bladder. He excused himself and went for a pee in the toilet of The Ranch for the third time that night. As he returned to the corner table and sat down beside Janine he was prepared to agree to pretty much anything she proposed.

"How can I help?" he said as he sat down.

"I need you to hide Rosie for a week or so until I can arrange somewhere for her and Carol to stay long term." Janine looked at George in the way that very few women had ever looked at him. In a way that said I need you and only you.

If George had ever been able to resist a request like that it had been a long time ago and had probably involved his mother during his primary school years.

"I promise to help you in any way that I can," said George, meaning every word of it as he stared into Janine's eyes.

"I knew I could count on you," replied Janine. "Can Rosie move in with you tonight until I can organise something more permanent?"

George stared into her eyes and realised he would agree to anything. "Only for a day or so," he replied, knowing that days, weeks, years didn't matter if Janine needed his help.

Janine put her hand on George's knee and squeezed it in a way he hadn't experienced for some time.

"I'll never forget this, George Milne," she said.

George knew that he would never forget it either.

"That's okay," he said as casually as he could.

Chapter Eighteen

George woke up in bed slightly earlier than usual without being quite sure why. There had not been any loud noise of any kind, no clatter of dishes or dropped cutlery but he was somehow aware of movement in the house. Then he remembered about Rosie moving in. For some reason this made him want to get out of bed earlier than he would otherwise have done. He got up and carefully put on his dressing gown. Then he walked through to the bathroom to have a pee. The bathroom looked and smelled clean. Most striking of all, the toilet seat was in the down position which George noticed just in time. After relieving himself he felt obliged to wash his hands and found a bottle with a dispenser cap sitting on the sink, primed and ready for the purpose.

Then he went through to the kitchen to go about the usual morning ritual of making his first cup of coffee. The kitchen was looking quite different to what he was used to. Gone were the piles of unwashed plates, cups and associated knives, forks and spoons. The sink was empty and clean. Very clean in the way that suggested cleaning products had recently been used. As well as all the dishes having been washed they had also been dried and put away in the correct cupboards.

There was also a certain smell about the place which was pleasant rather than stale and unwelcome. The flip top bin had been emptied and a fresh bag placed inside ready for the next items of rubbish. The bin lid had even been cleaned. Thrown for a second or two, he managed to find the necessary accoutrements for making the coffee but only after searching through drawers and cupboards and finding spotlessly clean versions of the items he would normally have used.

Once he had made his coffee, he took the mug and two digestive biscuits through to the lounge. The television was already on but not at the BBC news channel. Instead it was on a channel which showed a succession of noisy music videos. In fairness, Janine's daughter Rosie had the volume fairly low.

She was sitting in his favourite chair wearing a onesie in the pattern of a zebra, complete with a hood. In George's fairly sheltered life he had never before given a single thought to bestiality but looking at her he knew that he would never be able to look at zebras on the television in quite the same way ever again.

"Hi George," she said cheerfully. As she turned to face him with a smile he noticed that the front of the onesie was open sufficiently to display a large amount of cleavage. He tried not to stare at her breasts as they spoke and managed it for almost 50% of the time. Rosie was the most beautiful girl who had ever spoken to him and George was unable to avoid staring at her in utter awe. Her mother Janine had been a beauty at school and in her time was pursued by every boy in her year and the two years above and the one below. But Rosie was in a different league and she was sitting in George's house, on his favourite chair, watching his television, dressed as a zebra with cleavage, and somehow he didn't mind one little bit.

Chapter Nineteen

George's doorbell rang as he was about to sit down with a mug of coffee. He placed the mug on the wine table beside his favourite chair and walked to the door hoping it wasn't Frankie looking for an update.

When he opened the door there was a complete stranger standing there holding up a badge which identified him as a member of Police Scotland.

"Mr Milne is it?" said Jimmy Bell.

"Aye it is. What have I done?" asked George only half joking. In his school days George had developed an air of low intelligence whenever dealing with authority. His teachers found it difficult to scold him if they were not sure he understood what they were saying. It had served him well then and he found himself automatically reverting to it now.

"Oh it's nothing like that," said Jimmy. "I just wondered if I could have a wee word off the record."

"As long as it's off the record that's fine. Come on in," said George indicating the direction of the living room.

Jimmy followed George through to the living room and sat down on the sofa, eyeing up the fresh mug of coffee hoping he'd be offered one too. But he wasn't.

After George had settled into his own chair and started sipping the coffee Jimmy began his pitch.

"I'm a detective with the local cops. I believe you're a bit of a detective too. The big difference is that I track down rats rather than cats." He paused and looked at George, smiling at his own wit.

"There can't be that many people keep rats as pets, never mind let them escape," said George.

Jimmy started to worry that he was trying to enlist the help of a simpleton but he continued anyway.

"Not that kind of rat, Mr Milne. I track down the kind of rat that sells drugs to kids and beats them up if they can't pay or even try to kick the habit. The kind of rat that snaps people's fingers and toes off with hedge cutters as a warning but also for fun. The kind of rat that makes business rivals disappear overnight as if they never existed. In other words, rats like Frankie Cook. Is that a name you are familiar with?"

Jimmy stared at George to gauge his reaction and was disappointed to find there had been none to speak of.

"I just try to find cats for people, Mr Bell. A bloke called Frankie Cook called round the day before yesterday and asked me to find his sister's black cat which is missing. I'm going to try but there isn't much to go on. I am planning to visit his sister and get some more details."

"Is that the full extent of your dealings with Frankie Cook?"

"I've never dealt with anyone, never mind Mr Cook. He came here the other day to ask me to find his sister's cat. That is the only time I have set eyes on him."

"I believe you drink in The Ranch," asked Jimmy starting to feel either George Milne was an idiot or was taking the piss.

"I do. I play darts there every Friday and Sunday evenings. I'm not very good."

"Did you know that Frankie Cook drinks there all the time?"

"I've never seen him there," said George in all honesty.

"Well he does," said Jimmy angrily. Jimmy felt he was getting nowhere fast but from his years of experience realised that on balance, George was probably telling the truth.

"I would be grateful if you could keep your ears open during all your future dealings… meetings with this Mr Cook, especially if you visit his pad where the sister lives. To date he has been very careful in covering his tracks, usually by intimidating witnesses, but if you were able to get some kind of angle for me on his drug dealing or violent assaults, I could put him away for a very long time and make the streets of Coatshill much safer. Here's my card if you can help me at all with information."

Jimmy handed a business card to George who promised to help if he could, but repeated several times that he was only interested in finding Frankie's sister's cat.

Jimmy rose with a struggle out of the low sofa and shook George's hand then made his way to the front door offering to see himself out. George accepted the offer and continued to sit and finish his coffee.

Jimmy stopped on the threshold of the living room door, realising that he was not going to be accompanied to the front door, turned and said, "Sometimes life gives people a unique chance to do some good. It can be anyone and they may need to find courage they didn't know they had, but when they do it makes the world a better place. Goodbye, Mr Milne, and keep in touch."

George was not happy about the recent turn of events. This policeman had the look of someone capable of violence, a trait he seemed to share with Frankie Cook. George hated and was scared of violence, managing to avoid it most of his life. The only time he had come close to inflicting violence on someone else was that one occasion at school when he had told Glenda that Duncan Boyd had called her a fat cow. He had watched dismayed as Glenda knocked out one of Duncan's front teeth during a short and very one-sided display of aggression. Since then he had never been in or witnessed a fight. His two recent visitors appeared to be bringing violence to his door uninvited, and he was scared.

Chapter Twenty

George phoned the number Frankie had given him and waited for a reply. After five rings the phone was answered and a voice said: "What?"

It wasn't Frankie's voice and didn't sound like it could be his sister either.

"I wanted to speak to Evelyn Cook please," said George.

There was a whispering in the background and the handset must have changed hands.

"Who the fuck wants to speak to Evelyn?" asked the unmistakable voice of Frankie.

"It's George here, George Milne. I wondered if I could speak to your sister and get some more details about her cat."

"Aye, okay, I suppose so. You best come round to the flat though, she's no good wi' the phone. Give it an hour, I'm busy at the moment, then come round," ordered Frankie before slamming down the phone.

A few seconds later he had to pick up the phone again. "What?"

"Hello, it's George again. George Milne. Which floor are you on?"

Frankie swore and hit something in the background. George thought he heard a muffled groan but he couldn't be sure.

"Top floor, 10 Woodend fucking Walk," he hissed down the phone. "Remember give it a good hour before you come round." Again he slammed down the phone.

George knew the street well and reckoned it would only take about 20 minutes to get there so he put the kettle on and made himself a cup of tea to kill some time.

George arrived at the entrance to 10 Woodend Walk and looked up at the top floor flats. He had deliberately waited for over an hour to ensure that Frankie had concluded any business he had had under way at the time of the phone call. Looking at the ground floor flats he noticed a bald old man staring out at him through the front room window. George waved and smiled and the old man waved and smiled back while fiddling with something round his neck. A crucifix perhaps, George mused, and then took a deep breath, entered the close and climbed the stairs to the top.

There was a choice of two doors at the top of the stairs. One was a lovely period wooden door with ornate patterned glass between delicately beaded oak sections with a delicate knocker in the middle and a glass name panel at the side which read 'Blackery'.

The other door was made of steel panels and sat in a solid steel frame. It had no letter box or knocker, or bell attached and there was no name panel anywhere to be seen. That was unimportant, as all that steel and security had 'Frankie Cook' written all over it.

George knocked at the door and hurt his hand. It did however make a dull thud. A spy hole which George had not previously noticed shed a trickle of light through and this was followed by the unmistakable sound of large bolts being pulled back. The door then opened and the doorway was almost fully blocked by Willie McBride.

"Are you the cat guy?" he asked.

"Yes. George Milne, cat detective," replied George.

Willie ushered him to step forward and then almost immediately signalled for him to stop. Then George found himself subjected to a frisking which would have done justice to any airport's security arrangements.

"Can't be too careful. Know what I mean?" said Willie in a slightly friendlier tone when he had finished.

George nodded to be polite but didn't entirely know what he had been suspected of carrying.

Willie signalled for George to follow him through to the living room and there George met Evelyn Cook for the first time.

She was sitting on a couch watching Jeremy Kyle, and only vaguely acknowledged George's arrival. Evelyn was slim in an unhealthy way from lack of proper diet, exercise or regular fresh air and her skin was a pale, almost yellowy, colour. She sat with her hands clasped on her lap in front of her and stared straight ahead. Her hair was blond and in much better condition than the rest of her, as if she regularly visited a hairdresser or a hairdresser regularly visited her. The curtains were drawn, keeping the room quite dark, despite the heroic efforts of the low power bulb in the standard lamp near where Evelyn was sitting. The overall impression George got was of a young Miss Haversham in the early days after rejection, locked away from the world, crushed and not yet recovered enough to plot revenge on mankind.

Willie walked over to the television and switched it off without any words or signals to Evelyn who looked round when the television screen went blank without any suggestion she had been interrupted. Evelyn had known Willie all her life and regarded him as a second brother. He was always in or around the flat she shared with Frankie, and it seemed that this had always been the case. For his part, Willie regarded Evelyn as a sister and took his turn to look after her or look out for her when Frankie was otherwise engaged. They might as well have been brother and sister he thought. After all, if helping her brother kill their father didn't make him part of the Cook family, what did?

"This is George Milne, Evelyn. He's here to try and find your cat," said Willie in a very matter of fact way. "Tell him everything you can about Raven. Answer all his questions and don't leave anything out."

Evelyn nodded at Willie and turned to face George.

Willie headed for the kitchen and said to George as he left, "best of luck, mate."

George stared at Evelyn for a minute or two, surprised at both her good looks and her distance from events around her. After a pause he thought he better ask some questions.

"Your brother Frankie has asked me to find your cat Raven. I believe he is missing."

"Yes," Evelyn replied simply, suggesting this could be a long and difficult conversation.

"When did you last see him?" asked George.

After a pause suggesting great deliberation Evelyn replied, "The day the police came round."

"When was that?" asked George.

"I'm not sure, but Willie will know. He had to push at the door for a while till Frankie was ready," replied Evelyn.

"Okay I'll check with Willie about exact dates. Can you describe Raven to me?"

"She's black. All black."

"Have you any idea where she might have gone?"

"No," said Evelyn vacantly. "But don't let Frankie hurt her."

"What makes you think he might hurt her?" asked George.

"Because he killed my other two cats when they scratched him," replied Evelyn. "Snowball and PeeWee. I got a black one after that so that it could hide better."

George was slightly taken aback. "Surely Frankie wants to make sure Raven is okay?"

"Not really. He just wants the collar back cause he hid something in it when the police came round."

A penny dropped in George's consciousness and he felt a rush of fear throughout his lower body. He was already regretting drinking that extra cup of tea while he waited till the appointed hour for his visit. Now he was suddenly desperate for a pee and his bladder was refusing to wait.

"Can I use your toilet please?" he asked Evelyn who nodded and pointed to the hallway.

"Second left."

George stood up and sighed as the pressure was slightly reduced on his bladder. He followed the directions given, walked into the bathroom and locked the door. As he turned to the toilet undoing his zip as he went, he nearly urinated all over the floor in shock. In the bath was what looked like a small crocodile. It was staring at him with a hungry look which he found scary, despite the creature's size.

Regaining control he quickly completed the reason for his visit, all the while staring at the crocodile in the bath. Then he went back to the front room as quickly as he could.

"Did you know there was a crocodile in your bath?" he asked without thinking.

Evelyn looked at him with neither emotion nor interest.

"That's Rambo. It's Frankie's and lives there, but Frankie puts it in his bedroom when I need to have bath."

George stared at her for second wondering if the real world ever fully registered with her, then he decided to finish the interview as quickly as he politely could and then leave.

"Is there anything else you can tell me that might help me find Raven?" asked George with little expectation of hearing anything of use from Evelyn.

"He doesn't like milk," said Evelyn after a minute's pause.

"Thank you, Evelyn," said George trying to ensure there was no hint of sarcasm in his voice.

A hint of a smile floated briefly across Evelyn's face as George got up to leave but it kept floating and disappeared almost as quickly. Instinctively George switched the television back on and went through to the kitchen where Willie was watching a war film on another television there.

"I hope that helped," said Willie with no attempt to hide the sarcasm in his voice.

"Some," replied George.

"Frankie's getting annoyed that it's taking so long to find this cat. You better find it soon or he'll go loopy, and trust me, you don't want that."

George nodded, realising after this visit that his task had nothing whatsoever to do with a loving brother doing a kindness for his sister and instead had something to do with Wacky Frank's day job. As a result his heart sank as he was let out of the flat by Willie.

Old Miss Blackery was arriving at her door as he came out and was pleasantly surprised to get a polite "Hello" from someone leaving her neighbours' house.

"Hello," she replied and smiled at George. He smiled back wondering what it must be like to live next door to the Cook family and their associates.

As George exited the close of 10 Woodend Walk he decided he needed some thinking time and a walk followed by a few drinks at The Ranch to steady his nerves.

Chapter Twenty One

Jim Simmons was getting a little concerned. The agreed date and time for Frankie to take over his drug supply operations in Lanarkshire had come and gone. Already three of his best local contacts in Lanarkshire had phoned to say the number they had been given was unobtainable. More worrying for Jim was the fact that he couldn't get in touch with Frankie by mobile on the number he had used before. After two days, during which Jim had had to use his own people as before to fulfil orders, he decided to take action.

A phone call to a police officer he knew and paid frequently, confirmed that Frankie's house had recently been raided but that nothing incriminating had been found in the way of drugs or unexplainable sums of cash. There was the little matter of a baby crocodile found in Frankie's bath, but a lawyer had already visited and explained to the Coatshill police that his client had bought it in good faith, thinking it was a bearded dragon, and was shocked to discover the truth. The insider confirmed there was nothing else they could pin on Frankie or Willie McBride. He also confirmed, unprompted, that the surveillance operation on Frankie had been pulled for reasons of costs after the failure of the raid and that the two officers currently living on the ground floor of Frankie's tenement would be moving out that day. Jim chuckled to himself without any real humour and thought, what a world. Two coppers on one side of the entrance and Baldy Wilson on the other. You just can't trust anybody these days.

Jim put the phone down, both reassured and unsettled. He was reassured that Frankie was smart enough to live in a sterilised flat and had not been caught with any incriminating contact details of any drug network, either his own or Jim's new franchise. He was however unsettled that the police were aware of Frankie's activities, to the extent of being able to obtain a search warrant and raid his flat almost immediately after the new arrangement came into force. Somewhere along the line Frankie had been careless and now there was the possibility of that carelessness homing in on Jim himself. He decided he needed to think and so he headed for the hot tub in the leisure area of his house where he did all of his best thinking.

Jim's hot tub was in a conservatory-like structure to the rear of his property, out of sight of any public area. Through the bullet proof glass he was able to look outside to the patio and formal garden area to the rear of the building. Looking around inside he could take in the hot house, Japanese garden he had created with its bonsai trees, lush plants and bubbling water feature. He liked this part of his house. It was a soothing place to wash out the cares of the day or to relax and think through any business problems. Today he needed it for the latter purpose.

Frankie was an impressive little thug who had ambitions to join the big time. To date, he had avoided trouble with the police with the exception of a few minor offences relating to cannabis as a teenager. He had a tight organisation around him with a couple of enforcers who had a no-nonsense approach to cash flow which Jim admired. The plan to use Frankie to run Jim's Lanarkshire operations had been a sound one and perhaps still held good despite the police raid. Time would tell. Time however was not a luxury Jim had to spare. He had commitments to fulfil up the way and down the way, and ideally needed all his own team to safeguard his existing business in Glasgow itself. Frankie had been a quick fix for extra brains and muscle in Lanarkshire and a source of funds for the purchase of his bolt-hole estate in the Balkans. His own funds and Frankie's £1.5 million would secure it but he needed the cash flow to continue from all his businesses and Frankie's second tranche of money to pay the price in full. He was buying it from a Russian businessman in the same line of trade as himself and suspected that a late payment would go down very badly.

As he soaked in the hot tub with the bubbles circulating around him Jim decided the simplest thing all round was to give Frankie one more chance. If he didn't deliver his side of the bargain within the next week he would be removed from the business plan and Jim would just have to run everything as before until a suitable replacement could be found. If that happened he was sure Ben and Jerry could ascertain where Frankie was keeping the other £1.5 million and liberate it. That just left Jim £3 million short for his Russian seller but he could make that up one way or another.

With the decision made Jim got out of the hot tub and towelled himself dry. After putting on a thick towelling dressing gown he walked through to his study, typed in a number from memory and waited till the call was answered.

"Hi Callum," he said. "I want you to speak to Frankie Cook and ask him what the fuck is going on. Tell him to get things sorted by next Friday or all bets are off. Understood?"

"No probs," said the voice at the other end calmly. "I'll give him a bell right now."

Chapter Twenty Two

George again woke up before his usual time and for a moment wondered why. Again there had been no noise in the background, but he was aware of movement in his flat, and if he listened carefully, he could hear the sound of a television in his living room on but at a very low volume. As he came to, he remembered that not only did Rosie now live there but her friend Carol had also moved in. He put on the new dressing gown he had bought and walked through to the bathroom. It smelled its now familiar pleasant smell of Pot Pourri and perfume. He had got used to the seat being down, even when he was still half asleep and propped it upright before having a pee. When he was finished he continued with his new habit of washing his hands thoroughly using the scented soap dispenser on the sink. Before leaving for the kitchen he put the seat down and then washed his hands again.

Then he walked through to his immaculately clean kitchen and switched the kettle on. He collected a mug and a spoon from their allotted places then put a spoonful of coffee and a spoonful of sugar into the mug from the round metallic containers appropriately marked which had appeared from nowhere. He carefully replaced the lids on both containers and put them back in the line of similar containers before washing the spoon, drying it and placing it back in the teaspoon section of the drawer beside the sink. He took a sip of coffee and grabbed two digestive biscuits from the new pig-shaped biscuit barrel. Then he took another sip of coffee and sighed. Another day had begun.

George came through from the kitchen to find two young and impossibly attractive young girls sitting on the sofa in his front room. Both girls were wearing zebra pattern onesies of the kind he was now having difficulty ignoring.

He would have sighed if he didn't realise that this state of affairs meant that his favourite chair was again free for him, so he sat down and sipped his mug of coffee quietly for a moment or two.

After a second or so of very intimate hugs and kisses the zebras both looked up and, in a slightly embarrassed way wished George Good Morning.

George tried desperately to accept their greeting with the minimum of interest but there was only so much a lonely man could accept under his roof when it came to rabid female zebras .

He picked up his laptop and switched it on. As ever, it seemed to take ages to boot up but eventually did with the BBC News website as the main home page. George had largely given up the use of his own television and let the girls watch what they wanted. In a way it was no different to the arrangement he had endured with Glenda and her mother but in other ways it was so much better. Instead of a bad tempered size 22 and her equally bad tempered mother hogging the television set without any consideration of what he would have liked to watch and no active sex life as compensation, he now had the beautiful Rosie and her equally attractive friend Carol hogging his television. They would even occasionally ask if there was anything on TV he preferred to watch rather than their endless choice of soaps and reality TV. He would answer honestly that there was not. There was nothing on TV he would prefer to watch over watching the girls sitting on his couch watching TV. There was still no active sex life on offer but on balance there was a lot of other compensation in this arrangement.

After he had scanned the headlines and reassured himself that he was fairly up to date with what was happening in the world he logged on to Facebook. He didn't have many friends but there was a notification from one of them so he opened it. "Willie Taylor invites you to play pet rescue saga," it said. "Very funny," thought George. "Willie Taylor can fuck right off." With nothing else on the laptop to retain his attention he turned to his recently acquired pastime of watching Rosie and Carol while they watched his television.

A number of other major changes had occurred in George's house recently. Although the girls paid no rent, they did contribute to the food bill. Their main contribution to the household, however, was to clean and tidy the house to a standard unseen even in his mother's younger and more active days. There were never any dishes in the sink for days at a time now and every work surface in the kitchen was spotless and 99.9% germ free. Similarly the carpets were immaculately hoovered several times a week and all furniture free of dust. The television screen had never shown a clearer picture and all the insides of the windows were just as clean.

Of all the areas of the house to benefit from two women's touches, the bathroom showed the greatest transformation. Gone were the half used tubes of toothpaste and shaving cream with the lids left to one side. Gone too were the stains around every surface of the toilet bowl. Instead of the usual evidence of a bachelor's purely functional bathroom, George was now the proud owner of a sweet-smelling paradise of cleanliness: a palatial, self-contained, world of pot pourri and perfume. All obvious signs of basic male grooming were hidden away in the wall mounted cabinet, no matter how often George left them lying around. Every square inch of the room appeared to be cleaned several times a day. There was never any evidence of the girls' usage of the room and the toilet seat was always firmly down when George entered the bathroom. At first George had found this obsession with cleanliness disturbing but he had quickly come to like the smells and the look of this transformed room and started to look forward to his visits in a way he had never previously considered possible.

One thing that George struggled to adjust to was the range of clothing which appeared on the clothes drying rack above the bath. He had installed this 'pulley' years ago for his mother who used it to dry everything from shirts to sheets. George had continued to use it when he returned to the house for the same purpose. When the girls moved in, however, it regularly displayed clothes and underwear which would have had Mrs Milne spinning in her grave, if she hadn't been cremated. Some of the underwear only just qualified as such in George's opinion. Some of the girls' thongs would have been more accurately described as floss. He had declined the offer of having his own underwear washed by the girls out of sheer embarrassment at their style and condition, but he allowed them to wash his shirts. He would spend quite some time regarding the items on the pulley and contemplating how they must look on the girls before dragging his attention back to reality. They somehow represented a promise of erotic adventures in a world populated by beautiful young women. It was a different world, he would muse, and one which had largely passed him by over the years.

Chapter Twenty Three

Callum arranged to meet Frankie at the Bothwell services on the M74 just south of Glasgow. He had no desire to be seen at 10 Woodend Walk, especially so soon after a police raid, nor to be caught behind its steel door if Frankie or Willie decided to shoot the messenger. He was there well before the agreed meeting time and watched Frankie arrive in a non-descript Ford Mondeo rather than his usual Land Rover with its attention-grabbing blacked out windows. After a suitable pause to make sure he hadn't been followed Frankie went inside and sat down beside Callum, leaving Willie McBride behind as instructed.

"Jim's looking for an update, Frankie," he said in his usual friendly tone. "He hasn't been able to contact you by phone and some of his customers are getting worried."

"Tell him sorry about that," replied Frankie with an element of respect. "I had some trouble with the police the other day and I've had to lay a bit low but it'll be business as usual very soon. Tell Jim he doesn't have to worry. I had to hide the contact details for his people in Lanarkshire and now that the heat is off a bit I'll get them back and crack on."

"Jim heard about that. There were two cops on the ground floor watching you for ages. He knows that they have nothing on you and as a result the surveillance has been pulled. Apparently the cops involved are now engaged; how sweet. So what can I tell him?"

Callum had been on the fringes of the drugs business for years but had somehow managed to act as a freelance. He was as honest as any crook you could imagine and also delivered what he promised every time. He had worked on a day-rate basis for gangs in Glasgow and Lanarkshire for years and knew everyone who was anyone. As a result of his relative neutrality and experience he had been used as a go-between on more than one occasion. He was a messenger only. He would pass on messages in full, would then listen and report back to the other party in full. He walked quietly but carried no big stick of his own as it were. He was trusted with everyone's secrets and never betrayed them. Today he was there because Jim needed to get a message to Frankie and to hear the reply. Nothing more, and Frankie understood this.

"You can tell Jim that I have everything under control. I need two more days, then I will take up the reins again. That's a promise. Here's a new mobile number for me in the meantime."

"Two days including today?"

"No, two days after today, then I'm good to go."

"Okay," said Callum. "I'll pass that on."

With that both men left the café. Callum headed to the toilet in order to make a separate journey to the car park and Frankie headed to his car where Willie was waiting.

"How'd it go?" asked Willie with concern.

"We need to get a whole load of money fast and to find Evie's fucking cat, dead or alive. Next time you see that Milne character tell him from me to get his finger out, okay?"

"Aye Frankie I'll do that," said Willie. "In the meantime I've got a list here of who owes you the most. Shall I start my rounds?"

Frankie looked over the list and pointed at one name, "Bring that bastard round to the flat when you get him, for some personal coaching. You better get Spider onto it too. He can start at the bottom of the list and work up. I want lots of cash by the end of the week."

"No problem!" said Willie starting the car and driving towards the onramp to the motorway nearby.

Shortly after they left, Callum went outside and into his white van. He had an appointment to keep in Bearsden and didn't want to be late for it. His years of experience told him that the reply he was bringing wasn't going to be well received by Jim Simmons. He didn't care. It was Frankie's problem not his. After all, he was just the messenger.

Chapter Twenty Four

The following weeks saw George's life take a number of bizarre twists, all of which were completely out of his control.

Shortly after Rosie and Carol moved into his spare room he was sitting quietly on his favourite chair watching the News at Ten and trying to ignore the sounds of zebras mating emanating from his spare room when there was a quiet knock on his back door. At first he tried to ignore it but it kept repeating until he felt obliged to answer it.

When he did he was surprised and alarmed to find Frankie Cook standing there. Expecting imminent death he froze and managed not to react at all.

Frankie handed him a heavy suitcase and whispered, "I need you to hide this for a while. If you look inside you're dead, okay?"

George took the suitcase and nodded, then Frankie disappeared down the garden path.

George pushed the suitcase under his bed and returned to watch the coverage of a former African president's funeral.

A few nights later Frankie appeared again at George's back door this time with Evelyn and another, lighter suitcase.

"I need you to put Evelyn up in your spare room for a wee while. I might have some trouble to sort out and I want her to be safe. You're the only person I know who won't try to shag her. If you do, mind, you're dead." With that he disappeared down the garden path and into the darkness once more.

George wasn't entirely sure if he had been complimented or insulted by Frankie but he did know Evelyn was safe under his roof in that respect. He was also not sure if he or Evelyn was more confused by events but soon became aware that he was the more likely of the two to try to make sense of them.

"Come on in pet," he managed to say. "You're safe here. I'll put the kettle on."

The final phrase seemed to reassure Evelyn somehow and he managed to usher her into his flat and into the front room.

Rosie and Carol looked up in genuine amazement as George led a not unattractive woman through to his front room and sat her down on his favourite chair.

"Well, you're a dark horse," said one of the two zebras.

"Who is your lady friend?" asked the other in the same mischievous tone.

George looked round and, snapping out of his shock realised what they were hinting at.

"It's not like that," he countered vaguely with his mind lost on more important matters.

"Not like what?" giggled Rosie. "We're not suggesting anything untoward about a pretty lady friend arriving in the middle of the night with a suitcase and getting to sit in your favourite chair."

George thought through various cover stories he could make up or options of being economical with the truth and then thought to himself, "Fuck it!"

"This is Evelyn Cook, Frankie's wee sister."

The zebras stopped dead in their tracks as if a hunter had magically shot both of them simultaneously with the same, well aimed bullet.

"She needs to stay here for a wee while," George continued, taking advantage of the stunned silence. "And one way or another it will have to be in your room. Won't be for long hopefully. All we need to do is make sure Frankie doesn't know you are here too."

He turned to Evelyn who was staring at Question Time on the television in a fascinated trance. So much for Jeremy Kyle, George thought.

"Evelyn," he said quite loudly and out of the blue which attracted her attention away from David Cameron explaining how his government was going to help the poor of the country next. "These are my nieces June and… Joanie, who are staying with me at the moment. You will have to share a room with them but they won't mind sharing the double bed and you can have the fold down one in the corner. Is that okay Evelyn?"

Evelyn nodded and smiled at the two girls briefly before turning to watch Ed Miliband promise to defend Britain's poor from any more Conservative help while not actually promising anything much different. George suspected from Evelyn's face that she was a lifelong "don't know".

The girls had recovered a little bit of composure but still looked scared. Rosie had recovered enough to mouth "June and Joanie" at George in a way that said "Oh really?"

George shrugged his shoulders in a way that suggested he had come up with the first names he thought of while under a fair bit of pressure.

Rosie stood up with a look of resignation on her face and said, "Come on Joanie, let's help Evelyn to settle in."

Carol stood up and whispered under her breath, "I had hoped you were Joanie, June."

"No, no I'm definitely June because I got there first," said Rosie as her normal good humour started to return and she stuck her tongue out at Carol who slapped her bottom playfully.

"Come on Evelyn, let's get you sorted out," said Carol.

Evelyn didn't seem to hear her and remained staring at the television.

"Evie, sweetheart," said Rosie. "Come along with us."

When she heard the name Evie, Evelyn looked up with what almost looked like a smile and followed the zebras through to the bedroom.

George breathed a sigh of relief and returned to watch one of his favourite programmes.

"And I'm afraid that's all we have time for this week. Thank you to The Prime Minister…"

"Bugger!" George thought and headed off to bed.

The next morning after a restless night George came through to the front room as part of his usual morning ritual, carrying his personal mug of coffee to find three attractive female zebras sitting on his couch. Two of them were unashamedly hugging each other while the other, an older paler version of the other two, was watching a recorded episode of Jeremy Kyle on his television.

Rosie looked up and said, "I lent Evelyn one of my spare onesies so she would feel at home. What do you think?"

George wasn't sure his thoughts would go down too well in mixed company so he just smiled and said, "Very cute. You all match beautifully." Then he sat down in his favourite chair which he was relieved to find was still vacant.

Over the next few days Evelyn visibly relaxed in her new home for a number of reasons. She liked the company of George's "nieces" and they looked after her well. She was able to sit and watch daytime TV without loud interruptions from Frankie or Willie McBride or noises in the background as they had business meetings with clients or colleagues. Perhaps most of all she found George a safe, almost neutral, presence in the house. He would bring her tea or toast and ask if she needed anything anytime he went out but otherwise didn't try to force conversation or leer at her the way some men had, Richard in particular. Perhaps that is what fathers were meant to be like, she wondered vaguely. He also called her Evie, which made her feel safer still.

As a result she actually initiated occasional conversations with him, generally about whether or not he was enjoying Jeremy Kyle. George usually was not and generally read rather than watched it with her but he would always make some kind of friendly comment. Evelyn liked that.

On one occasion as George finished a chapter of his book and put it down to rest his eyes he said to her in a concerned and friendly way, "I'm afraid I haven't found Raven yet."

At the mention of her cat's name Evelyn looked round at him with a quizzical expression on her face.

"You won't find him," she said matter-of-factly. "He's hiding where I showed him to hide so that Frankie doesn't hurt him."

George looked at her and kept his friendliest possible face on. "That's clever of him. Where does he hide?"

Evelyn wanted to help George but she was afraid he would give Raven to Frankie and then he might hurt her like he had Snowball and Pee Wee when they had scratched him.

"If I tell you, do you promise me that you will only take her collar off for Frankie and not let him hurt her? That's all he really wants."

"I promise you that if you tell me where Raven is, I will take her collar off and leave her there, safe from Frankie. I like cats too, you know," he lied to her with his best fatherly smile.

"Okay then," said Evelyn, reassured. "This time I got a black cat and showed it the hole in the panels at the back of the hall cupboard one day when nobody was about. I pushed a wee bit of her blanket through the gap so she would know it was her special place. Frankie built a cat flap on my window so she could go in or out without him having to open the front door and she can jump from the roof of the shop next door to use it."

She smiled as she said it, feeling very clever with herself.

"After the police raid she came back. She'll be in the cupboard. The new woman on the ground floor promised to feed Raven if I was ever away."

With that she turned back to the television, apparently finished saying all she had to say.

George stared at her in amazement. Maybe at least some of her difficulties were an act. A defence mechanism developed at an early age to deal with a horrific childhood. "Who knows? " he thought. But at least he knew one thing now: Where Frankie's sister's cat was hiding. Another successful result for the cat detective.

He was about to go and make himself a mug of coffee when he thought he would try for one last piece of the jigsaw while Evelyn was in a chatty mood.

"Evie. What did Frankie hide in Raven's collar?" he asked in the same fatherly tone.

"The fish and chips from his phones," she said. "He wants them back so he can talk to his friends again. Otherwise they might fall out with him."

"Thanks Evie," said George. "Would you like a nice cup of tea, and as you've been really helpful you can have one of my chocolate digestives with it."

She nodded and smiled. George smiled too, but not at the thought of a cup of tea and a chocolate digestive. All of a sudden he had a bit of leverage over Wacky Frank Cook.

Chapter Twenty Five

The whole idea of George going to a speed dating evening had been Willie Taylor's. How he had managed to talk him into it he wasn't sure. But Willie had a way with words and George was slightly tempted by the possibility of some pleasant female company if things went well. When the subject was first raised at the darts session on the Sunday before the event itself George had initially dismissed it out of hand.

Gordon had laughed and said, "At your age?" Before apologising, when he saw the look on all of his friends' faces.

Raymond had been dead against it. "Some people just don't know when they are well off. You've just escaped one miserable situation and now you want to jump back into another. You'd be off your head to go."

Jock was unsure what a speed dating evening was about but didn't want to demonstrate his ignorance on the subject. It sounded to him like George had to shag a lot of women in succession and take the best one home. Beyond that he didn't see the problem as long as suitable precautions were taken all round.

Janine listened from behind the bar for a while before chipping in her thoughts on the matter. "You don't need to be going to something like that to find yourself a good woman."

Before George could assimilate that comment Willie countered, "Nothing ventured, nothing gained, my man. There must be lots of women out there gagging for the attentions of an experienced formerly married man like yourself. Get yourself along there and pull. These things always have more women than men because men get embarrassed. Single women just get desperate."

Janine snorted as she stifled a laugh and wandered off to find something behind the bar to polish.

The conversation had continued in much the same vain until George eventually agreed to "give it a go," mainly to shut Willie up.

Thus committed he had found that his name and personal details had been entered online by Willie Taylor, probably after he got home that same Sunday evening. As a result a delegate pack arrived through the post with a list of descriptions of the female attendees but no pictures and no names. The descriptions suggested he might be going back stage at The Miss World contest. In fairness, had he known, Willie had described George in terms that had some of the ladies expecting to meet George Clooney.

Despite all the stress and trauma of the week before, or perhaps because of it, George kept his promise to his fellow "Ranchers" in the darts team and attended the speed dating evening. He had spent some considerable time grooming himself and preparing his best suit for the occasion. A shirt had been freshly pressed and a tasteful tie selected. Shoes were brushed to a match the rest of the ensemble and, following a thumbs up from two out of three of the zebras, at seven o'clock he headed out to The Ranch for a swift one to steady his nerves.

"My, my you do scrub up well, George Milne," said Janine as he entered the bar. "I only wish it was my night off and I would save you a trip."

She winked after she said this and George felt again a feeling of warmth rise up within him.

"A pint of heavy," said George trying not to go red.

"You don't want to arrive smelling of drink," said Janine. "Women hate that at a first date, trust me."

George looked confused not really sure what else to have.

"I'll make you a cup of tea if you like, on the house," Janine offered, rescuing him.

The other darts players arrived and made various comments about George's turnout, both good and bad.

Willie Taylor felt duty bound to support their man, having persuaded him to go in the first place. Raymond was still adamant that the whole venture was doomed from the outset. Gordon was still laughing about it and Jock handed George a packet of 12 condoms with a knowing nod of the head.

Janine returned with two mugs of tea and handed one to George.

"Looking forward to this, are you?" she asked George.

"Not really," George admitted. "I just feel obliged to go through with it because I promised Willie. He seemed very keen. I feel a bit silly now though."

"I don't think it's silly to try and put the past behind you and look for somebody new," said Janine looking straight into his eyes. "This might not be the best way though. Anyway, time is moving on and you'll be late if you don't go now. If you don't pull come back and tell me all about it. I'll buy you a drink."

George nodded, finished his mug of tea and headed towards the door with a variety of cheers and comments following on behind.

As he got to the door Willie Taylor shouted, "Good luck! Anyone has got to be better than Glenda, eh?"

As George entered the Lesser Town Hall, collected his badge and table number and looked round he saw

Glenda at the same time as she saw him. Her jaw dropped and she turned away immediately. George kept his jaw in position but only just. They both looked down at the list of names they would be meeting and saw with horror that they were due to meet first at table seven. Then both of them looked up and without saying anything, almost telepathically, agreed to miss out round one of tonight's speed dating.

That had been a bad start but it got worse as George realised that both of Glenda's bridesmaids were listed, her mother and five other staff from Franny's Bakery. He was about to turn and leave when one of the organisers, an impossibly positive woman called Georgina, linked her arm through his and steered him towards a table laden with glasses of Cava.

"Help yourself to a drink, young man," she said. "We have a feast of possibilities for you tonight."

George would have used the word 'probabilities', all of which were bad, but the idea of a drink of any kind suddenly appealed. He took the glass she handed him and watched as she floated off to prevent any others of faint heart making a run for it. He drank it in one go and grabbed another. This was going to be a long evening if they didn't allow him to escape.

His initial feelings of dread at reading the list proved to be well founded. Although both he and Glenda had sat out the first round, literally, by hiding in toilet cubicles, he was dragged back by Georgina and there was no escape from the rest of the evening.

The ladies from Franny's bakery had obviously been curious to meet him after Glenda had pointed out the bastard who had ruined her life. Her mother was less forgiving when she sat down in front of him at table seven to give him a piece of her mind. The bridesmaids followed suit.

In between these combative rounds there were a number of other candidates for George to try to consider: a lady of 40-something called Linda, who made Glenda look quite slim, one called Lesley, who may not have eaten anything for ten years or so, and several others who George suspected had not told their husbands the true purpose of their night out. In the midst of all this hatred and desperation George found himself sitting next to a lovely woman called Susan. There were no surnames on the badges they had been given so it was just Susan. She had given her surname as Haig or Hay or similar but George was too busy admiring her figure to catch it. She was probably in her late 40s and had looked after her figure well. Having divorced her husband she had focussed on raising their only child on her own. Now that her daughter was away from home and working, Susan had decided to find some happiness second time around and this evening was the first toe in the water.

George listened to all of this personal detail and stared at Susan. He mumbled some answers to her questions about his own circumstances and smiled a lot. He could not find any flaw in this candidate. She was lovely. She was also slim, sensibly nourished, funny and intelligent. He was about to think that the night might not be such a waste of time after all when he realised that Susan kept checking her watch for the time and was obviously desperate to find somebody more interesting than him. When Georgina finally rang her little bell Susan was off like a shot to be replaced immediately by Glenda's larger bridesmaid who was clearly a woman on a mission at table seven; another piece of someone's mind was coming his way, whether he liked it or not.

Chapter Twenty Six

After the raid on Frankie Cook's flat, Jimmy Bell had had to endure endless jokes from his fellow officers regarding the details. Having the door opened voluntarily by Willie McBride had been a bad start. Finding nothing incriminating beyond a baby crocodile had sealed the result in the minds of his colleagues. Thereafter he became the victim of endless jokes both funny and banal regarding crocodiles. Would this be an open and shut case; just like the croc's jaws? Did he have a thick skin to survive the jokes? No crocodile tears from anyone regarding Frankie's spoilt evening. "It just went on and fucking on," he thought. Pictures of crocodiles (and some, inaccurately, of alligators) appeared on noticeboards throughout the Police Headquarters building in Coatshill. Email jokes were circulated endlessly and on one occasion, a child's inflatable crocodile was suspended above Jimmy's office door.

The raid on Frankie Cook's flat had not been a success. In fact Jimmy Bell concluded that with the cost involved, the diverted manpower and the expectations raised with his superiors it was something of a failure, in the same way and on the same scale as saying the Titanic's maiden voyage could have gone better. He knew there would be a reckoning and he knew it would involve an interview without coffee with Superintendent Murphy. Murphy was an astute political policeman with high hopes of making it to the very top of the policeman's ladder. For him each operation was either a tick in the box for future promotion or a black eye. Whenever it was a black eye he would show a boxer's ability to dodge it and have the blow land on one of his subordinates. If a tick was achieved he would make sure that the credit ended up on his report card. "Spud" Murphy had carved a successful swathe through his contemporaries' ambitions and reached the rank of Superintendent rather quickly as a result. He had allowed Jimmy Bell a lot of leeway and funding for operation "Woodend Waltz" and it had not produced the results he had hoped for. A major drugs bust in Lanarkshire was way overdue and he had hoped this might be a breakthrough. Instead, it had soaked up a lot of money, embarrassed him in front of his Glasgow colleagues and produced a small crocodile. He wanted to make it crystal clear to all concerned that the blame lay entirely with Jimmy Bell and his obviously dodgy intelligence. From a career point of view the first stage of this was to have an interview with Jimmy which would leave him in no doubt that he must do better and do it with no further extra funding.

Jimmy sat outside Spud's office cursing under his breath. He knew, as did Spud, that Frankie was the key player in Coatshill's drug culture. Everyone on the street knew that if you snorted, injected or smoked anything inside the burgh limits of Coatshill you had better have bought it from Frankie. There were even tales of people bringing their own stuff home from holidays and paying "corkage" to Willie McBride as a result to stay healthy. Somehow Frankie had been ready, or was tipped off, or maybe was too clever to be caught this time round, but Jimmy felt he had got close. Frankie's card was marked, and maybe even this Simmons guy the Glasgow squad were interested in was too. If nothing else they had caught Frankie keeping a dangerous animal without the necessary licence. At least that was something.

"Come in!" bellowed Spud, and Jimmy entered the lion's den. "Don't say one fucking thing about that crocodile, understood."

"Yes sir," said Jimmy, aware he had no further cards to play.

"I don't want to dwell on the past," lied Spud. "But your raid on Woodend Walk was a fiasco. A failure of the first order. You found no drugs, no unexplainable cash and no telephone numbers of contacts. Instead you found a small lizard and one of your female officers is now suing the force having been scratched and bitten by a traumatised cat, whose owner may still sue us for psychological damage to the animal involved. In addition, a past offender with health problems had the emergency link to his neighbours severed without authority. Do you have anything to say in mitigation?"

Jimmy had been hoping to mention the crocodile at this point but decided, on balance, this would be unwise.

"No sir," he replied. "We were unlucky this time. He's the source of all drugs in Coatshill and if he is in cahoots with Jim Simmons then he has extended his claws further afield. It is only a matter of time before he slips up, sir."

"No Jimmy, you were wrong this time, not unlucky, and that will be recorded on your file. We don't have time to dedicate good officers to an investigation which produces no results. I want you to go out there and bring me somebody's head. Anybody's. Frankie fucking Cook can wait. Perhaps sooner or later an opportunity will arise to throw the book at him but until then I want people jailed. Jailed for possession, jailed for dealing, jailed for holding small quantities of anything or even looking a little bit suspicious but I want results is that clear?"

"Yes sir," said Jimmy trying to sound more obedient than pissed off.

"I want you to jail so many underlings that the whole edifice collapses and brings down one of the big fish. I want to see Frankie Cook or someone similar fall from a very great height. Now go and do your job, Sgt Bell, and catch me some drug-abusing felons."

Jimmy left Spud's office on something of a low. He had been that close to catching Frankie but something had gone wrong outwith his control. They had searched the flat with the proverbial fine tooth comb and found nothing. He had even phoned Edinburgh Zoo to see if crocodiles could be given an enema. But there was something festering away at the back of his mind and he couldn't quite place it. Spud had brought it back to the fore but in the embarrassment of the interview it had disappeared. What was it he wondered? Then it hit him like a bolt. The fucking cat was the only thing to have left the flat without being searched in every orifice. Maybe it was time to pay another visit to the cat detective.

Jimmy Bell walked up the garden path to the front door of George Milne's ground floor flat with determination in every step. The interview with his boss, Supt. Spud Murphy was still fresh in his mind. He had no intention of locking up dozens of drug users to satisfy Spud's wounded pride and damaged career prospects. Ground feeders were of no use to him and would make no difference to the misery that drugs inflicted on his patch. No, Jimmy wanted a big scalp or preferably two or three and somehow Frankie's cat held the key. As Sherlock Holmes had once said, "When you have eliminated the impossible, whatever remains, however improbable, must be the truth." Jimmy had read all the Sherlock Holmes stories, had watched every Sherlock Holmes film and had even bought a deerstalker, though he had never plucked up the courage to wear it in public. He did however have aspirations of greatness as a detective, and not a fictional one at that. If he could put Frankie or Simmons and their teams away he would be talked about in police stations the length and breadth of Scotland. That would be reward enough for him and if he did he would make damn sure Spud didn't steal all the credit. Either way, this Milne guy knew more than he was letting on and Jimmy was going to make him reveal what he knew one way or another.

When Jimmy arrived at the front door he decided to give it a good "policeman's knock" and scare everyone inside rather than use the doorbell. The door shook dangerously on its hinges and after a few seconds it was answered by a gorgeous young woman in a zebra onesie. This vision of beauty was enough to throw Jimmy for just a second before he gathered his composure again.

"I'm looking for George Milne, is he in?" asked Jimmy staring unashamedly at the zebra's cleavage.

"Not at the moment," Carol replied. "He's gone out."

"Do you know when he is likely to return?" asked Jimmy managing to look Carol in the eye. Behind Carol another zebra, at least as beautiful as the first, made its way to the kitchen waving at Jimmy as it went followed seconds later by another whose hood was up but whose figure suggested yet another beautiful creature. What the hell has this Milne guy got going for him, he wondered, apart from an unnatural fascination with animals?

"I'm afraid not," replied Carol. "I'm afraid he has abandoned us again with no details of his plans."

Jimmy was pretty sure he would not have abandoned the zebras without good reason but did not get drawn on that point.

"It's very important that I speak to him. I need to ask him about a cat."

"Have you lost your cat?" asked Carol in all seriousness. "George is good at finding cats. He's a cat detective."

"No of course not," said Jimmy irritably. "It's somebody else's cat. To be honest I don't like cats." Then he added quickly, "Of course I like other animals."

"Especially zebras," thought Carol as she closed the upper part of her onesie to allow Jimmy to better focus on his work.

Jimmy took the hint reluctantly and handed over his card.

"Please ask him to phone me as soon as he gets back. I need to ask him about Raven."

"Is it a cat or a raven your friend has lost?" asked Carol trying not to laugh.

"It's a cat called Raven. George knows all about it. Tell him it's vital that I find that cat," shouted Jimmy as he headed back down the path towards his car. How many fucking zebras are there in there, he wondered, and what were they and Milne up to?

Chapter Twenty Seven

Mr Wilson lived on the ground floor of 10 Woodend Walk and to the casual observer looked every bit the standard-issue harmless pensioner from central casting that he tried to appear. For those who knew him better he was Baldy Wilson who had spent 37 of his 72 years in a variety of Scottish prisons.

He was one of life's followers and never a leader, and as a result, while he had never actually harmed anyone directly himself, he had been sent down with some of the most violent criminals of his time. Inside prison he had acquired a hard-won reputation as a poor fighter and had been beaten and thumped so often that his hearing, speech and general health were very poor. As a result he had eventually retired to a flat which surprisingly had been purchased legitimately along the way, and thereafter lived a quiet life.

To all intents and purposes he was a largely disabled old buddy whose daily highlight was the visit from his carer, who cooked some food for him and ensured he was otherwise comfortable and well turned out. If anyone had noticed the panic button round his neck or the large red button on the side of his chair they would have assumed that it provided 24 hour emergency assistance should he need it. They would however, have been well off the mark. Both buttons were instead connected to a well-concealed thin wire which ran from the rear window of Baldy Wilson's flat to the rear window of Frankie Cook's flat on the top floor. Combined with a one way glass panel in his front door and some prisms fitted in Baldy's windows the buttons helped ensure that nobody could visit Frankie unannounced.

As a result of this arrangement Frankie had generally never been caught unaware by either his rivals or the local police, with the exception of Jimmy's recent and unfruitful visit. In return Frankie kept Baldy in cigarettes and drink and arranged for the occasional visit by a carer of a quite different type.

One Tuesday evening the doorbell rang at Baldy's flat. He got up and answered it at a speed which would have amazed both his doctor and his team of carers. He didn't recognise the well-dressed figure he could see through the door and as a result answered it without thinking.

"Remember me?" asked Gentleman Jim Simmons as the door opened.

One foot blocked the door as Baldy tried to slam it shut and after a neat dance step the other tripped him up as he tried to make it to the panic button in the hallway. As he fell Jim grabbed at and removed the one attached to Baldy's neck.

Baldy suddenly remembered who Jim was, and the small detail of helping one of his rivals when he had initially set up shop in Glasgow. It had been a few years before and Baldy had rather hoped that little indiscretion had been forgotten about. The people he had worked with at the time had come a very poor second to Jim's internationally backed team when they tried to resist the new order. Some members of the main family had died in a house fire and Baldy had had to lay low for a while. It was largely due to that set of circumstances that he had finally retired to the flat in Coatshill. Unfortunately for Baldy, Jim had a very good memory and a totally unforgiving nature.

"Now, now. Let's not spoil the surprise of my visit, eh?" he added as one of his team passed him and dragged Baldy Wilson toward his final visit ever to his own bathroom.

Jim Simmons turned and climbed the stairs behind the rest of his cohorts, intent on a quick and decisive visit to the dump others liked to call Coatshill.

At the top of the stairs Jim played his master stroke. One of his waitresses, Sheena, bore a striking resemblance to Rosie McGovern and with some careful dressing and coaching was ready to open the door for Jim and his team. Callum had become aware of Frankie's infatuation and had passed on the information to Jim. Unable to locate Rosie at short notice but aided by a photo Callum had taken some time before, Jim had been able to set a tempting trap. Sheena knocked as hard as she could on the steel door, terrified to do anything else and stood in front of the spyhole. When a chink of light appeared she smiled as best she could and said, "It's Rosie. Is Frankie there?"

The spyhole closed briefly and then the door opened to show Frankie standing there in surprised confusion. His surprise and confusion didn't last long as the door was forced wide open and Ben, Jerry and Jim rushed in. Sheena turned sadly and walked downstairs again to sit and wait in one of Jim's Range Rovers, feeling guilty at her role in Frankie's demise, but relief at being alive and still having her looks.

Ben and Jerry tackled a spirited assault by Willie McBride in a way which would have been the envy of Police Scotland. They then neutralised a pointless charge by Frankie and were thereafter relieved to find that Spider was not in the flat. Willie was dumped in the bath with a slash across his throat and Callum held him down till he stopped moving. Frankie was floored with no regards for his human rights and dragged back to the front room in front of Jim in a stress position that even George Bush Jr. and Dick Cheney would have regarded as torture.

"Well, well, well," whispered Jim as Frankie was paraded in front of him. "I am very disappointed in you, Francis. I had hoped you were up to the little task I had set you, but apparently not."

Frankie eyed him with undisguised hatred. "It's Frankie ya bastard, no Francis."

Jim watched unconcerned as Ben inflicted a massive blow to Frankie's face.

"I assume it will come as no surprise to learn that our little business arrangement will be terminated today," continued Jim. "I have to tidy up a few issues and suggest you cooperate if you wish to shuffle off your mortal coil with relative ease. Let's start by you telling me where the balance of the £3million is - I have rather promised it to some colleagues of mine who are as fastidious about late payments as I am."

Frankie looked him in the eye and realised that Jim was essentially in the same boat as him but on a grander scale. The irony might be the last pleasure he would experience but by Christ he would milk it if he could.

"Sorry old bean," he said, mimicking Jim. "I am afraid there never was another payment in my coffers. I bluffed you, and now you're fucked too."

Ben and Jerry let fly for a moment or two on Frankie while their boss thought things through.

"So you never had the other one and a half million quid?" he asked speculatively, but already aware of the answer.

"No chance, you daft fucker. I was going to take it out of Lanarkshire over the first three months, one way or another."

"I see," said Jim, indicating to Ben and Jerry to stay their hands for a second while he thought things through. He wished he could go and soak in his hot tub with time to reflect but immediately dismissed the notion.

"Okay, partner," said Jim now staring straight into Frankie's eyes with malevolence which his henchmen had never seen before. "Today is the last day of your life. We both know that and nothing can change the fact. Your only choice is the manner of your…. demise. I am going to ask you a few questions and I suggest you answer them very accurately or we may have to continue this discussion somewhere remote and in Ayrshire."

Frankie just stared back with a grin that only a psychopath with bravado could manage. Ben took a large pair of secateurs out of a pocket somewhere inside his coat while Jerry kept Frankie in a firm grip. At a signal from Jim, Ben lopped off one of Frankie's fingers. He cried out in pain, then stifled it as best he could.

"I want to get my mobile SIM card back so that I can give it to somebody who is not as fucking stupid as you," said Jim. "Understand?"

Frankie laughed a mirthless laugh and spat back through broken teeth, "The joke's on you then, you fucker. I don't have a clue where it is."

Jim was unhappy with that answer and nodded to his Polish colleagues who continued to use the secateurs on Frankie. Deep within his head though, Frankie realised that Evie's greatest hope was to stay at George's house and for George to remain a mystery to the Glasgow gang in his flat even though the suitcase of money that George was hiding could have given him some sort of bargaining tool. As the minutes and pain increased he shouted and swore, but said nothing about his sister or her protector, George Milne.

Eventually Jim called a halt to proceedings and indicated for Ben and Jerry to get rid of Frankie once and for all and then search the flat. He had no great hopes of finding anything but felt the need to go through the motions while he was there. Ben and Jerry opened the front door and threw Frankie over the bannister. Then they closed the door and set about as detailed a search of the flat as they and Callum could manage against a tight timescale.

Five minutes or so after Frankie's last flight there was a knock on the door. Ben was nominated to answer it and was surprised to find a meter reader going about his everyday business. Callum had heard the meter reader saying a farewell to the old lady next door but his arrival at Frankie's door took them all by surprise. Jim indicated to Ben, whose English was better than Jerry's, to get rid of the unwelcome visitor, but try as he might Ben could not get him to take the hint. Callum kept his usual low profile, which was just as well for George on this occasion. Eventually when mention was made of calling the police, Jim signalled for Ben to allow the meter reader in. Had he strayed off the straight line between the front door and the hall cupboard where the meter was he would have been a dead man but he seemed focused on his work and took the shortest route to the meter concerned and left after a few minutes in the cupboard. As soon as he was gone, Jim ordered a further quick search of the flat before the whole team beat a hasty retreat back to Glasgow.

On the return journey Jim mused to himself that things could be worse. He had Frankie's £1.5 million, and no obligation attached. He was free to try to milk Lanarkshire for the balance of payments for his property purchase without any interference and that area could now include Coatshill if he was quick. The manner of Frankie's death would leave his customers in no doubt about the nature of their new supplier. The nagging doubt in the back of his mind, though, was the missing mobile phone SIM with the Lanarkshire contacts on it. If a reasonably smart copper got hold of that it could spell a major problem for his business before he could relocate to the Balkans. After a few minutes of the journey home he reassured himself that the chances of any copper, let alone a reasonably bright one, getting hold of the SIM were slim. With his wife comfortably sunning herself in the Bahamas he turned his attention to Sheena sitting beside him in the Range Rover.

"I have to say, sweetheart, I was very impressed with your performance today. I feel it only fair that we go back to my place and celebrate."

Sheena smiled another forced smile. "Shit," she thought to herself. "I'm not off the hook yet."

Chapter Twenty Seven

George walked up to the door of The Ranch wearing his best suit for no reason in particular. It still had the badge from the speed dating event pinned to the lapel. He hesitated in the doorway for a second wondering if this was such a good idea. Asking Janine out was a big step, and after the disaster at the Lesser Town Hall the night before he was reluctant to experience any more blows to his confidence.

Before leaving the house he had been able to convince himself that he should try his luck with her. Nothing ventured, nothing gained, kept ringing in his ear, in Willie Taylor's voice. The suit seemed appropriate as he put it on. After all Janine had said, "You do scrub up well." It had to improve his chances. Now though, on the threshold of walking into the pub his confidence and resolve had evaporated. As he stood there, seriously considering going back home, he was aware of raised voices coming from inside.

He put his eye to one of the small transparent sections of the window next to the door and peeked through. The Ranch was empty apart from Janine behind the bar and a man of average height and build on the customers' side. They were having a really heated argument about something and for a second George wondered if it was Janine's ex. The man's hands were resting on the brass rail of the bar and George could see that his knuckles had letters tattooed on them. He could only see one clearly and it read "hate". He assumed that the other hand had "love" written on it. But he was wrong. There was nothing approaching love anywhere in Spider's make up.

Putting his ear to the glass he could just about make out what they were saying.

"Tell me where she is and nobody needs to get hurt," said the tattooed man. "She is going to go out with Frankie sooner or later. He doesn't take no for an answer."

"You two better leave Rosie alone," shouted Janine in reply. "I'll kill anyone who hurts her."

At that, Spider reached across the bar and grabbed Janine by the neck with his left hand. "Tell me where that little tart is, you fucking bitch, or I'll tear your face off."

With his right hand he picked up a pint glass from the counter and smashed it against the bar.

George was terrified but was more concerned for Janine and her lovely face. He wracked his brains for some kind of weapon from the contents of his suit and came up with nothing. Through the window he looked around for something inside that he could use. There was a tray from the glass washing machine on the bar and it had more pint glasses in it. He didn't rate his chances in a fair fight with Janine's attacker using only a broken glass, even if he made it far enough to grab one. He had never used a glass for anything but drinking before and Spider looked like he used them for assault or beer, turn about. Then George noticed the credit card reading machine on the end of the bar nearest the door. It would have to do.

Without fully thinking what he was doing he gently but quickly pushed the door aside, grabbed at the card reader and swung it down on the back of Spider's head with as much force as he could muster. Spider had heard the door open too late, and although he had started to turn his head he wasn't quick enough to see the blow coming. As the edge of the card reader caught him behind the ear he released both Janine and the broken glass he was holding in an instinctive jolt. Pain surged through his head but he didn't black out. George had followed through and now swung again, hitting Spider across the nose. This blow had no apparent effect, this part of his body having been hit so often before. He now turned fully towards his assailant with sheer anger flashing in his eyes.

"Shit," thought George. "He's still upright."

George stared at Spider's face and assumed that a violent and painful death was imminent. However, just as he braced himself for Spider's retribution there was a huge explosion of roasting hot coffee at the back of Spider's head and he slumped forward and collapsed onto the floor unconscious. Behind the bar, Janine was standing with only the handle of a large catering coffee jug in her hand. Her face was ashen but full of resolve.

"I'll phone the police and tell them what happened but leave you out of it," she said. "You better leg it before they arrive. Hopefully the police will keep him out of circulation for a while and he'll be a bit hazy about what actually happened."

George nodded, still in a combined state of shock and relief.

"Oh, and thanks George Milne. You're my hero," Janine added with a smile.

George gathered his thoughts and decided this was a turning point from which he couldn't look back.

"All in a day's work," he managed to say returning the smile. "Now, if you'll excuse me, I have a cat to find."

Janine watched him leave the pub with a look of bafflement on her face. He really was a strange guy, she thought to herself, but he had come up trumps a few times recently when she needed help most.

She turned to look at the unconscious figure of Stevie "Spider" Webb lying bleeding on her newly cleaned floor and decided he might bump his head one more time before she called the police.

Chapter Twenty Eight

George made his way to 10 Woodend Walk with no
clear idea of what he would do once he got there.
Somehow he needed to get into the flat and somehow
he needed to find Raven and get the microchip out of
his collar. After that he would decide what to do with
it. He thought it unlikely that Frankie would be
overwhelmingly grateful and simply pay up and walk
away. Ultimately, though, he had to decide which
option was most likely to keep Frankie away from
Rosie and now Janine.

As he got to the entrance to the close of number 10 he
looked to see if the bald old man was looking out and
smiling back but there was no sign of him through the
downstairs window. There was however a Range
Rover with blacked-out windows parked near the
entrance and the driver eyed him suspiciously. George
smiled at him with a cheery nod as if to say you don't
have to worry about me and then went inside and
started up the stairs. When he reached the first floor
he could hear raised voices coming from above. None
of them sounded like old Miss Blackery so he
assumed Frankie had visitors. From the sound of the
voices they included some Polish guests.

He was about to head back down the stairs and return at a more opportune moment when there was a scream and couple of shouts. Something was thrown over the bannister from the top floor and passed George at speed, heading in freefall down the stairwell. As the object passed him, George saw that it was a rather bruised and battered Frankie Cook. For a split second their eyes met and George had the impression that Frankie was pleading for help. Later he was sure he had imagined it. Either way Frankie continued his descent and landed at the foot of the stairs with a thud and squelch.

George pushed himself back against the wall in fright; desperately hoping that whoever had thrown Frankie off the top floor couldn't see him on the floor below. Whatever had taken place above, it was likely that if Frankie had come to a sticky end then big Willie McBride had preceded him and George didn't want to tangle with whoever had got the better of him.

George stood there for a moment trying to breathe as silently as possible. After what seemed like an age but was probably only a minute or two he heard footsteps heading back into Frankie's flat. He reckoned it must now be safe to head down the stairs and out of number 10 and hope he never met any of the people above again, either socially or unsocially.

As he got his breath back he realised that he was still holding the credit card reader from The Ranch. He must have carried it in his hand all the way without realising it. Apart from a small speck of blood it was none the worse for connecting with Spider's head as a weapon. Looking at it and looking at the badge on his lapel from the speed-dating event suddenly gave George an idea. Instead of going down stairs and running as far away as possible from the carnage he had witnessed he found himself calmly climbing the remaining stairs to the top floor. His movements had an unreal dreamlike quality about them. One voice in his head was screaming to run away while another calmly told him to keep going upstairs, everything would be okay. George was wishing the first voice would win. He knew however, that to protect Janine, Rosie and himself would require action sooner or later. Let's finish this now; the second voice seemed to be arguing and there was a certain attraction in that course of action.

As he reached Miss Blackery's door he paused and then, speaking very loudly, as if to someone who was deaf he said, "Thank you for the tea Miss Blackery. I'll see you in another six months."

Then he turned and walked to Frankie's door and rapped it hard three times with the card reader. There was a pause and he could hear muffled voices inside but nobody answered. He knocked the door again slightly louder and this time he noticed the spyhole being used. He smiled and pointed at his badge.

There was another pause before the door eventually opened. A huge figure blocked most of the doorway and asked, "What do you want?"

George again pointed at his badge and held up the card reader, "Electricity meter," he said as calmly as he could.

Ben stared at him before saying, "It's not a good time right now."

George stood there defiant, "This is the first time I've got you in in five visits. I really need to get a true reading."

Ben didn't move. "It is not a good time right now," he repeated.

"I'll just be two seconds. The meter is in the hall cupboard behind you."

"Not now, thank you," said Ben firmly.

George couldn't believe who was making the decisions in his head that day but it didn't appear to be him as his bluff continued. "As you are clearly in and your account is so far in arrears, I will need to call the police now so that I can get a reading today, unless you let me in yourself."

George smiled, "Neither of us wants that hassle and paperwork. Ten seconds in your cupboard, then I'm off."

There was a pause and a whispered instruction in the background.

Ben smiled a wide, stage smile, "I'm sorry I didn't fully understand. Come in and take a reading."

George walked smartly across the hall and opened the cupboard door, then he went inside and down on his hands and knees hoping all the time that no one grabbed him from behind and strangled him. Reaching round to the right hand side at the back he found the gap in the panelling just as Evelyn had described it. He reached through and winced as Raven immediately sank her teeth into his hand. Fortunately he had been expecting that and managed to grab at her collar, securing a tight grip first time. He gave a sharp tug and the collar came through the gap, no longer attached to the cat. He quickly put the collar into one of his jacket pockets and then carefully crawled backwards out of the cupboard.

He turned to Ben with a smile, "All done here."

Making a point of staring straight ahead he walked smartly to the front door.

"See you in six months," he shouted over his shoulder as he made it to the top of the stairs and as calmly as possible started his descent. He could feel a pair of eyes watching him as he went until Frankie's door slammed shut above him.

He continued down and started walking out towards the daylight. He noticed in passing that the bald old man's door was slightly open and he wondered if he was alright. He didn't stop to check though, deciding he would leave being a good neighbour to Miss Blackery or the police when they turned up.

He walked out of the close and onto the pavement. The driver of the Range Rover eyed him up again but George just smiled and nodded as before and walked swiftly away till he had turned the corner and was out of sight. At that point his legs turned to jelly and he started gasping for breath as relief spread throughout his body. He forced himself to recover though and quickly crossed the next road and headed down a back lane he knew from his days as a paper boy. From there he took a long route home, making sure every few minutes that nobody was following him.

Eventually he arrived at his house and let himself in with his key. He looked round for any sign of trouble but saw none. Everything looked exactly as it had when he had left earlier that day. As he began towards the kitchen a zebra appeared gracefully from the spare bedroom.

"Fancy a cup of tea?" Carol asked. "Rosie had to go and see her mother. Apparently there was some trouble at The Ranch today."

George nodded and headed for the front room dripping with sweat from the afternoon's exertions

"Cup of tea would be great thanks," he shouted through as he sank into his favourite chair and started watching Jeremy Kyle with the zebra on the sofa.

Chapter Twenty Nine

Frankie Cook's funeral was a strange and rather badly attended affair. For a man who had been so well known in and around Coatshill, his death had encouraged few to mourn or even celebrate his passing. Jimmy Bell had decided to attend to see if any felons appeared out of the woodwork and he had another two officers in civilian clothes to mingle with the mourners to see what intelligence could be gathered. The press decided to attend in quite generous numbers, with contingents from the Coatshill Courier, STV, BBC Scotland and all levels of Glasgow's newspaper industry. Glasgow's Red Top tabloid made a big thing of having the inside track on the local drugs gangs and their conflicts and decided to run a week's worth of salacious stories of violence and death at the hands of local villains. Frankie's funeral on the Monday of that week started the series off nicely. Supt. Spud Murphy had caught a whiff of potential publicity and decided to attend in full uniform, complete with The Queen's Police Medal. He was interviewed by all the press and somehow managed to put a positive spin on Frankie's demise, as if the police themselves had removed this hardened criminal from the public domain.

Jimmy watched his boss being interviewed, the press attending and realised that his undercover officers were wasting their time, even if they managed to mingle unnoticed by the 12 or so genuine mourners. Jimmy also looked round the small group at the graveside.

Frankie's sister Evelyn was there of course, in a new black outfit which rather suited her, and she was attended by a few younger female friends drawn from Franny's Bakery and the staff of The Ranch where Frankie had been a regular. The barmaid of The Ranch was there out of respect to one of her locals no doubt. Two other locals from the pub made up the remainder of the group. Old Jock was interviewed by most of the press looking for some detail of Frankie's exploits. He was happy enough to ramble on for ages about Frankie buying rounds for everyone in the pub, but as it became clear he had no knowledge of his criminal activities each interviewer quickly lost interest.

When Jimmy noticed that the other regular was George Milne, the fucking cat detective, his interest was aroused and he walked over to stand beside him.

"Terrible business," said Jimmy.

"You mean the drugs business?" asked George.

"I meant Frankie's murder, but maybe for once you're spot on. Did you ever get your hands on his cat?"

"I got my hands on it right enough but it scratched me and got away," said George, relapsing automatically into his obtuse mode as a defensive mechanism.

"Pity," said Jimmy. "I think it had some secrets to tell, one way or another."

"Aye, you can learn a lot from cats and Raven was no exception. They maybe don't say much but they watch everything going on. If they could talk we would learn a lot."

Jimmy looked at George starting to seriously think he was an imbecile after all.

"Of course sometimes they can tell us a lot without talking."

Jimmy was starting to lose the will to live and was about to go and chat to Old Jock when George added. "The secrets aren't always words at all."

With that George reached into the pocket of his coat and brought out an envelope which bulged slightly in the middle and handed it to Jimmy.

"I hope this is of use but you never got it from me mind," said George and walked over to put a fatherly hand on Evelyn's shoulder.

Jimmy shook the envelope gently and he heard the unmistakable ringing of a small cat bell. He put it in his pocket and headed away from the grave, got in his car and drove straight to the station.

By the time Spud Murphy had returned to the Police headquarters and changed out of his formal uniform Jimmy had examined the contents of the envelope and realised the potential of what he had been handed. Inside the small barrel beside Raven's bell he had found the two SIM cards from Frankie's phones. Technical branch had recovered the names and numbers from them within half an hour, and from scraps of intelligence already held, Jimmy realised that he had the numbers for all the main dealers and distributers, not only in Coatshill but Lanarkshire too, with a trail that led to Glasgow and possibly Jim Simmons himself. It was clear that some disruption to distribution of drugs had occurred recently across the county but the police had no clear idea of what or why. Maybe Frankie needed these SIMs and had hid them in the cat's collar when the police raid started. If that were the case and he never managed to retrieve them, that would explain the interruption to supplies. It could also explain Frankie's demise at the hands of an unimpressed business associate, maybe even Gentleman Jim Simmons himself. If all that were true and the Glasgow police could pen Jim and his team in for a while so they couldn't make alternative arrangements for phone contact, then perhaps he could track the people down from their mobile phones and get enough incriminating evidence to put a few of them away. Not the lowest of the low, but some of the real players in Lanarkshire.

Jimmy was waiting outside Spud's office when his superior arrived from changing during a rare lunch at home with his wife.

"Can I speak to you sir?" asked Jimmy with a look that suggested to Spud it was going to happen anyway.

"I hope you have something worth hearing this time, James," Spud replied.

"Oh, I think you're going to be rather interested in some info I picked up at Wacky Frank's funeral."

"Really? Impress me," said Spud.

Jimmy outlined in great detail the amount of information contained in the two SIM cards and the potential to track down and arrest a large number of major players in the Lanarkshire drugs industry. Jimmy emphasised the need for both speed and cooperation with their Glasgow colleagues. While he listened to the details Supt. Murphy imagined the press conference after his men, led fearlessly by himself, had put away some of the worst criminals in Lanarkshire if not the world.

Jimmy could see he was on to a winner by the look in Spud's face.

"If we run with this quickly enough, sir, we can put some more of these bastards away," the word more playing to Spud's earlier theme of Frankie's death being a police success, and struck a chord.

"I like what I'm hearing James. Tell me where this information came from. I need to know that it is 100% kosher."

Jimmy was ready for this.

"The SIMs were given to me by another detective, working on unrelated cases who realised the value of them to our operations. I cannot divulge his name for security reasons but I can confirm that the SIMs were recovered from Frankie's phones and are the real deal."

Spud stared at Jimmy for a second or two.

"I am prepared to put my full weight behind this to get phone taps, searches and the full cooperation of our colleagues in Glasgow but I expect big results this time, and if you don't get them I will hang you out to dry. Understood?"

"Yes sir," replied Jimmy recognising the usual, "heads Spud wins, tails someone else loses" offer of help.

"Obtain whatever resources you need," said Spud. "Any problems getting whatever you ask for refer it to me and good luck."

Jimmy left Spud's office on a mission. He was going to use the SIMs to track down every drug dealer or supplier in Lanarkshire worth the title and hand some more over to the Glasgow police at the same time if he could. Anyone who wasn't locked away for years would have their neck breathed down for years to come. Sherlock fucking Holmes eat your heart out.

Although Jimmy saw Spud as an over ambitious, self-promoting bastard, he had to admit that on this occasion he acted swiftly and with impressive organisational skills. Liaison was established again with counterparts in Glasgow who made life very difficult for Jim Simmons and his boys. This made it almost impossible for them to re-establish links with their customers in Lanarkshire via face-to-face meetings as they would have preferred. Instead they had to use the existing mobile phone numbers even if there was a strong danger of those being compromised. As a result the two police forces were able to gather massive amounts of information and lots of names, rapidly filling in huge gaps in their previous intelligence.

After three intensive days and armed with search warrants for a dozen different premises, the police swooped in a series of coordinated raids. They recovered large quantities of heroin, cocaine, amphetamines and cannabis, along with small amounts of a whole range of other drugs. In total they also recovered over half a million pounds in cash which would end up in some proceeds-of-crime charity effort somewhere doing good. Jim Simmons was not caught or provably incriminated. Ben and Jerry, however, were found with some cash, some drugs and a baseball bat covered in the blood of a recently discovered corpse, pulled out of the river Clyde that evening. In all, charges were successfully brought against 17 members of drug gangs in Lanarkshire and eight in Glasgow.

Supt. Murphy appeared over and over again on TV along with his opposite number in Glasgow, extolling the virtues of cooperation within Police Scotland and making sure that he was firmly associated in the mind of everyone who cared with this significant success. He even made a point of personally thanking Jimmy and hoping that the detective responsible for recovering the SIM cards was enjoying similar results. Jimmy thought of all those zebras and was pretty sure he was, one way or another.

Chapter Thirty

On one of the jetties at Inverkip Marina, Jim Simmons calmly loaded ten suitcases onto his sailing yacht, none of which contained clothes. Once he had finished he drove the dark blue Audi estate back to the car park and locked it with the remote control. As he slowly walked back to his yacht he threw the car keys into the water after checking that nobody was watching him. Before getting onto the boat he looked at the other boats around him. He then looked at the hills, the sea and every bit of Scotland that he could see taking in every detail that he could as if collecting memories to reuse in the years ahead. Which, of course, was exactly what he was doing. He would miss Scotland, he knew. The years back here had been good to him. He had even put on weight. But now he had to leave and move on. Although he was sad about this, in other ways he was excited by the future. He had phoned Grigori about the difficulties he had experienced since the Police got hold of his SIM card and after a brief reminisce over old times they had arranged everything. Jim would sail from Scotland towards Denmark and Grigori would arrange for a Russian ship to meet him at sea. After he was safely on board with his travelling funds, the ship would head for Hamburg where Grigori would meet him. They would have a wild night or two there just like old times and then head for Berlin. Once there Grigori had an opening which Jim might just find attractive enough to stay this time. Jim had had to admit that a night out in the bars and brothels of Berlin beat a night out in Bearsden any time, no offence to Bearsden.

Jim untied the yacht and took one last look round the marina. He looked at the Audi in the car park. He had never been fond of that shade of blue anyway. They did a really nice ochre colour now. He'd buy one of them in Berlin. Maybe the four wheel drive version. Yes, endless possibilities were opening up. He remembered a scene in a W C Fields film.

"Stranger, when I came to this town I had nothing but a sack over my shoulder and now I own every shop in the main street," Fields boasts.

"What was in the sack?" asks the stranger in awe.

"Two million dollars son; two million dollars."

Jim knew how he felt.

Chapter Thirty One

Although George had personally seen Frankie Cook fall to his death from the top floor of 10 Woodend Road and had attended his funeral, he was still reluctant to look inside the suitcase that Frankie had left with him. It could contain anything at all, he reasoned. Drugs, money, both; even the severed head of a rival's favourite racehorse for all he knew. The racehorse option was unlikely but with Frankie nothing could be ruled out. As a result the suitcase lay under his bed where he had hurriedly placed it, surrounded by George's own luggage, such as it was, to ensure it wasn't immediately visible.

As the days and then the weeks passed, he became less worried that someone might appear to claim it. Frankie was dead, Willie was dead and the tattooed man was under arrest in hospital, still in a serious condition. It was unlikely Frankie would have told anyone but Willie about it voluntarily. If he had mentioned it under duress then somebody would almost certainly have collected it by now, but no one had. Slowly but surely George gave in to curiosity. He waited exactly two months to the day after Frankie's funeral and then, having drawn the curtains in his room he pulled the suitcase out from under his bed.

It was an old battered item which had seen better days and probably warmer climates, but it was sound enough and the locks at each side still functioned perfectly. George had made his plans well though, and had laid out beside him a hammer, a chisel and assorted screwdrivers. After only two medium taps on each lock, the case was ready to divulge its secrets. George stared at the closed case for a minute or two, still nervous about opening it. Then he decided the damage was done, literally, and he would no longer be able to deny looking inside if anyone subsequently called to collect it. Then, after taking a deep breath, he opened Frankie's suitcase.

George had speculated for some time as to what might be inside and was prepared for most things. As a result the contents were almost an anti-climax: almost . Once open, the case revealed bundle after bundle of grubby used notes. They were mainly twenties and tens but there were a few smaller bundles of five pound notes and in a pouch on the lid he found a total of 30,000 Euros and a passport with Frankie's picture in it but in the name of David Gillespie.

He closed the lid again and just sat there for 20 minutes wondering what to do. This was obviously Frankie's getaway case. If things got dangerous he could grab it, scarper and lie low with enough cash to survive for a while. But things had got too dangerous too quickly for Frankie and he hadn't had time to take the money and run. Question was; would he have mentioned it to anyone at all? After thinking it through George decided that he probably wouldn't have mentioned it to anyone. This was the ultimate option of last resort. If anyone knew they would be able to swipe it or to track down David Gillespie Esq. as he travelled the globe. Willie McBride would have been the only possible confidant and, if so, he appeared to have taken the secret with him to an early grave. There was Evelyn of course but if she had ever known about it she had never mentioned it to him. No, this was Frankie's little secret and now nobody knew about it but George.

That brought George to the next question: What to do with the money? He could be an honest citizen and hand it in to his good friend Det Sgt Jimmy Bell, who would no doubt ensure it made its way to the proceeds-of-crime scheme. There it would fund football strips for disadvantaged kids or perhaps a sanctuary for abandoned greyhounds. George wasn't quite sure what was supported by the scheme but he was pretty certain it wouldn't include him. The more he thought about the last few weeks since he first met Frankie Cook the more he felt that Frankie owed him. On a basic level, George had taken in Evelyn and provided her with free board and lodgings. That probably added up to a fair bit less than was in the case, but it was a start.

While he thought about it further George decided to count the money and find out exactly how much was there. This took him some time. Time was money, he mused for no great reason, and chuckled. After well over two hours, he calculated that the case contained £497,540 plus the Euros. That was a lot of board and lodgings, he thought to himself. Perhaps Frankie had wanted George to have the money should anything happen to him so that he could look after Evelyn. It was a long shot but there was nobody about to argue against it.

Having counted the money George felt more of a sense of entitlement to it than he had before. He had now touched each note and placed them in piles. He reassured himself that had the sum been greater than, say, half a million pounds he should probably hand it in; but it was just below that critical level (ignoring the Euros which didn't really count somehow). He decided to round the total down to £497,000 by pocketing £540. This might make it easier for him to come to a decision about what to do with the money. Now that he was in funds to a rather generous extent he could go out to The Ranch, have a few beers and think things through properly.

At The Ranch George found that Rosie was working instead of her mother, allowing him to concentrate on the burning question of whether or not to keep Frankie's money. With none of the other players about, George was free to practice at the dart board all evening. This achieved two things. Firstly, he began to throw the darts better than he normally did when playing with the Friday and Sunday players. Secondly, he could think through all the options carefully, without the interruption of banter from his friends or conversation with Rosie who was chatting away to Carol between serving customers.

George decided that there were basically three main options. He could hand all the money into the police and know that he had helped several good causes. This course of action would right the wrongs done by Frankie when making the money in the first place. The police would be happy and George might well get some of the cash as a reward, money he could spend with a clear conscience. No doubt Jimmy Bell would thank him profusely and his superior would again appear on television and in the newspapers boasting about their most recent success in removing the ill-gotten gains of yet another criminal master mind.

The second option was to remove some of the cash to ensure that Evelyn would be okay in the years to come, largely by ensuring that George was okay in the years to come. After all, she had no one else now to look after her, so the job fell to him by default. This option was perhaps the trickiest of them all. He would have to decide at the outset, how much he would need to cover all eventualities, remove it and then hand the rest in. Thereafter, he would have to make the amount removed do, irrespective of what the future held. If he didn't take enough then there was no chance of returning later for more funds. There was also the possibility that the police might suspect what had happened and keep an eye on him from then on. They might even search his flat. He would then need to have a very safe hiding place which he could still access whenever necessary. If by any chance one of Frankie's former colleagues did know about the stash and saw that only some of it had been handed in, they might come after George or poor little Evie, looking for the balance. She had been through enough without bringing this possible danger to her door. Poor girl. On reflection then, George could pretty much reject this course of action as being too risky.

The third possible plan was in many ways the simplest and the safest. George could keep all the money. This way he would be able to care for Evelyn to the full extent of her brother's prudent financial planning. There would be no danger of the police keeping tabs on George or any criminal with inside knowledge of the suitcase. He had to admit that some worthwhile causes would lose out on a bumper dividend from the proceeds-of-crime scheme but he felt that was a price he was willing to pay. He could even make occasional voluntary donations to local good causes to compensate. As a statement of intent in this matter he popped a 50 pence piece into the charity box on the bar when he had paid for his next pint. The box was for animal welfare. Not his first choice perhaps, but the principle was sound. The next donation would be for sick children or similar to redress the balance. That assumed of course that George chose option three, and he had still not fully made up his mind.

The night wore on and the beer took its inevitable effect. George's ability at the dart board fell away as a result. He still felt his mind was clear though and able to come to the best decision regarding the money but he resolved to sleep on it for another night. His mother had brought him up to be an honest boy and he had reached a stage of inebriation where he remembered and missed his mother dearly. He knew that she would have expected him to do the honest thing and hand the money into the police.

"Honesty is its own reward," he could hear her say and briefly felt tears well up in his eyes.

This weighed heavily on his mind as he bade farewell to Rosie and got into the taxi she had organised for him. "Yes, he would sleep on it that night," he thought to himself but he could hear his mother's voice in his head telling him in her familiar, calm tones to do the decent thing. Tomorrow he would make the decision whether or not to keep the money. As he staggered up the garden path to his home he already knew what he would have to do.

Two days later, sober and well-dressed George had decided to take Evelyn out for a run in the new car he had brought with the first tranche of Frankie's money he had taken from the suitcase. Somehow, having Evelyn as the first passenger in the second-hand Ford Focus he had treated himself to, gave it an element of legitimacy. The memories of his mother's lessons in honesty had not survived the night as he slept off his evening of darts and deep perusal. In the morning, with a slight hangover, he had quickly decided that the safest and most sensible course of action was to keep the money and spend it slowly and wisely ensuring Evelyn's health and wellbeing from a position of greatly increased personal comfort.

Evelyn was, as far as one could tell, excited at the prospect of a trip in the car with George. Her trust in him had grown following Frankie's death and the unlikely survival of Raven due to his brave actions. She could not remember ever going on a car journey for the simple reason of a day out. George had even asked her where she would like to go. She had not had any ideas initially but after a few questions they had decided to visit Edinburgh Zoo to see the animals there. In the end George had suggested this and the idea of seeing a selection of different animals had been a clear winner.

Armed with a new camera, Evelyn had dressed up in some recently purchased clothes, chosen by her adoptive sisters, Rosie and Carol. She was ready long before George was, but waited patiently while he went through his usual morning routine as quickly as he could. Soon though, they were all fed and watered and headed off for the adventure that only a trip to a zoo can offer. George had considered inviting Janine to join them but was still unable to pluck up the courage of asking her out. He would do, he thought, it was just a case of working up to it and building up the mental strength to cope with the possible rejection he might receive. As a result of his lack of courage, today was limited to a rare treat for Evelyn visiting the zoo, an opportunity for him to get used to driving a car again and in addition, an occasion to salve his conscience regarding the decision he had taken on the future of Frankie's cash.

As they walked round the zoo together Evelyn held his hand. At first he found this a bit embarrassing. He was a good bit older than her and she was a lot better looking than he was. He wondered what people would think. After a while, though, he stopped caring and realised that Evelyn needed the reassurance of holding his hand. She had been through a lot in her life and had lost everyone who was actually related to her, as well as her surrogate brother, Willie McBride. She held George's hand in the way that a much younger girl would have held the hand of her father on an exciting but slightly scary adventure. In turn George realised that he was the nearest thing to a benevolent father figure she had ever known. She walked round the zoo in a constant state of thrilled bewilderment, pointing out all the different animals she saw along the way as if George might otherwise miss them.

"George, look at the monkeys. George look at the zebras," and so on. She even claimed to have seen Rambo on show at one point. George was sceptical about that one but Evelyn was insistent, so he smiled at her and nodded, not wanting to spoil the moment.

It would have grown a bit annoying after a while if George himself had not been enjoying the visit and the fact that he had female company for the first time in years, albeit nobody could have described it as a date. It was also nice to get away from Coatshill for a day and have the freedom to drive anywhere he wished.

George had passed his driving test when he was 17, at his father's insistence.

"If you have your health and a clean driving licence you'll always get work," he had said.

Shortly after passing his test, George wrote off the family car one night when he misjudged a surface on an icy corner. After apologising profusely from his hospital bed, George had vowed never to drive again. Although the insurance covered the cost of a replacement car, his father was not keen to let George behind the wheel of the new car and as a result it became an understanding that George wouldn't drive again till he bought a car of his own. This he had never done until investing Frankie's money, being able to walk to work each day or get a lift from a colleague or take a bus if it rained. Later during their marriage, Glenda had regarded cars as both expensive and dangerous and they provided a little bit too much freedom for any husband if they could walk to their work anyway.

George was a bit rusty therefore behind the wheel of the car and drove with the caution of someone who had recently had a bad accident. Evelyn had rarely been in a car in her life and on the few occasions she had been, found Frankie or Willie McBride's getaway style of driving quite frightening. In contrast she liked George's cautious approach far better. It all helped the feeling of safety she felt when she was with him.

Chapter Thirty Two

Over the years no further clues as to who had killed
Richard Pettigrew turned up until one Steven "Spider"
Webb was rushed to hospital after threatening the
barmaid of The Ranch pub. During the altercation he
had been knocked unconscious by the woman he had
threatened and was injured to the extent of being
rushed to intensive care. There, one of the police
officers posted to take a statement and who had been
on the search for Richard's killer years before,
recognised the ring on Spider's finger. The case was
reopened and, as Inspector Menzies had retired, it was
handed to Jimmy Bell. After a long conversation with
Menzies, Jimmy rushed round to the hospital.

David Harvey walked into the A&E department ready
for another gruelling shift. When he saw Jimmy Bell
sitting in the waiting area his mood did not improve.
Jimmy's presence meant only one thing; some local
crook had put a member of the public or another crook
in hospital.

"I take it we have some poor punter hospitalised by
one of the local criminal fraternity?" he asked Jimmy
in the usual world-weary but friendly tone he adopted
for the purpose.

"Strangely enough, this time round one of our local public has put a criminal into intensive care for a change. Striking a blow for the little guy, or in this case, the little barmaid."

"Wonders will never cease," said David. "What's your interest? Are you charging her with GBH?"

"Not yet, but I wouldn't rule it out. He seems to have banged his head on the floor of the pub a few times when he fell but we're not pursuing that line of enquiry. I am not at liberty to divulge the nature of our enquiries at this stage but, off the record, I want to talk to him about the ring he's wearing and what happened to the finger that wore it before him. Give us a shout if he comes round, mate."

"Will do! Is it a 'when' or an 'if' he comes round? "

"Could be either at the moment but you'll know better than me once you've read the notes."

David headed for the intensive care ward and started to read the medical notes for Stephen Webb who had been brought in by ambulance following a disturbance at The Ranch Bar. There was considerable damage caused by a number of blows to the head and severe scalding to the rear and right hand side from hot coffee. In the middle of the scalded area was a lesser blow which contained fragments of glass from a catering size, glass coffee jug. Mr Webb had been unconscious when he arrived and his condition had not changed since. Although he had been stabilised there was a chance he might not survive. The main danger to life was a deep and narrow hole through the left side of his skull caused by striking a protruding nail on the floor of the bar, according to the notes provided by the only witness at the time. The scribbled notes from the paramedic who had brought him in suggested the alternative of a lady's stiletto with a question mark after it.

David looked at the patient who lay lifeless on the bed. Even if he had not been a doctor he would have been fairly certain that Mr Webb was unwell. There were generous quantities of cooling gel which had been applied to the scalded area for a start. A variety of dressings covered the various results of numerous blows to the head. His pallor suggested the possibility that he was already dead but nobody had noticed. His professional reading of the details on the monitor to which Spider was connected confirmed that he was in fact still alive, if only just. The overall impression David got was of an extra being made up for a horror film who had been left half way through the process by the make-up team who had popped out for a tea break. The tattoos with "HATE" on each set of knuckles didn't sit comfortably with the "return of the mummy" look though. He decided there was little chance of any imminent recovery or opportunity for

Jimmy to question him any time soon, so he returned to the waiting room to let the policeman know.

"Okay mate," said Jimmy. "There's my card. Give me a phone if there is any change. There will be an officer on duty till he recovers."

"Could take a while if it ever happens," said David, "but will do."

Jimmy made for home desperately tired and ready for an early night, if his wife and kids would let him. David went back to the office to see who else was still in intensive care since his last shift. One of the baseball bat victims from his earlier shift on A&E was still hanging in there as was the old lady from the same night who had fallen and broken her hip. The hip had been replaced and things were going well till she developed MRSA whilst recuperating in one of the hospital wards. As a result she was now in intensive care and her chances were 50/50 at best. "At least do them no harm," chuckled David without any humour.

Spider remained in the same condition for weeks. Each day the doctors would check his vital signs or lack thereof and advise the nursing staff to continue doing whatever they had been doing as, to date, it hadn't killed him.

Much to everyone's surprise, Spider opened his eyes one day and briefly looked round. It was an action which would have been missed had one of the nurses not been in the process of changing his drip at the time. She tried to gain further response by talking to him without success and so she summoned the duty doctor to report what had occurred. Over the next few days the same thing happened again for slightly increased periods each time. Eventually Spider regained consciousness for several minutes at a time. David had been considering whether it was safe to inform Jimmy Bell of this turn of events when he appeared in the hospital, having been alerted by the officer on duty.

"I want to talk to him the next time he comes round," he told David. "Has he said anything?"

"Nothing at all so far and we have no indication that he is aware of his current situation or even his own identity yet. He hasn't responded to any form of stimulation."

"I'll soon stimulate him," whispered Jimmy under his breath as he side-stepped David and made for the intensive care bed where Spider was lying with his eyes firmly shut, oblivious to all the concern for his welfare.

Three hours later Jimmy admitted defeat. "Call me if he ever makes any sense, okay?"

"That was always my plan," said David under his breath and got on with his rounds.

Over the next few weeks Spider made slow progress but still showed little sign of response to the questioning of the medical staff and none whatsoever to Jimmy's efforts. The various drips and other attachments reduced in number as he began to be conscious for long periods and was able to take some nutrients orally, but still he seemed unable to speak or answer even the most basic of questions.

One night after Spider had been transferred to a room at the side of one of the main wards the police officer on duty heard him cry out, called the duty sister and ran to Spider's bedside. He was lying there with his eyes open but no other sign of consciousness. The nurse checked his vital signs, which were all exactly the same as before, shrugged her shoulders and went back to her form filling. The police officer waited beside the bed for any further developments but after an hour or so, with the patients eyes now closed, he too gave up and went for a coffee.

For his part Spider had, over the last few days, started to recover some of his lost memory. He realised he was in a hospital and knew instinctively that the police officers he became aware of were not there for his benefit. He said nothing although he felt that he now could. He was very weak and still in some pain but he had no real idea of what had happened and how he had ended up in hospital. Then in the middle of one quiet night he had a sudden recollection of standing in The Ranch bar with Janine McGovern and of her hitting him with a jug of boiling coffee. The pain had been excruciating but she had done nothing to help stop his suffering. He vaguely remembered her swearing at him and hitting him again before all went blank. This vision created such a rage in him that he had cried out. He was then aware of a policeman and a nurse rushing to his bedside. He lay there deliberately still and quiet till they went away again, all the time trying to piece together any other fragments of recent events. He sensed there had been someone else in the bar but could not recall who. There had been a man there too but he could not put a face to the figure. This man had maybe hit him too, but try as he might he could not summon any more details. Not to worry though, he had remembered enough. Janine fucking McGovern, a barmaid, had put him in hospital. That much he now knew. If there had been any lack of focus in his recovery before that night it had gone as he plotted revenge. Three nights later, while the duty police officer drank a coffee and failed to chat up one of the nurses, Stevie "Spider" Webb disappeared from the hospital without a trace.

Jimmy Bell was apoplectic with rage and spent a full 20 minutes telling the officer concerned what he thought of him. Worse still, Jimmy had to endure a similarly uncomfortable 30 minutes with Spud Murphy.

A massive man-hunt was set in motion as soon as Spider's escape was discovered but over the next few days police could find no sign of him. He had few known associates who were still alive and not in custody, and raids and surveillance failed to turn him up at any of the addresses the police tried. As a precaution, an officer was dispatched to guard The Ranch and its manager as she was the main witness to Spider's threats there. She was also the main reason he had been apprehended in the first place and come under suspicion of the murder of Richard Pettigrew. It was not unreasonable, therefore, to think he might seek her out, looking for revenge.

After a week when business levels plummeted at The Ranch, Janine had asked for the police presence to be scaled back from the two uniformed officers standing outside the front door. Reluctantly this request had been agreed and a vehicle patrol parked itself on the road near the front of the pub instead. Slowly but surely the locals, with the exception of Callum, began to return in numbers, all promising to protect Janine from Spider if necessary.

"Just let him show his face here," said Old Jock, "and I'll floor him myself. Honest Ah will."

Others offered similar support, some even offering to move into the Ranch until Spider was safely in custody. None of this made Janine feel particularly safe but she was reassured to know that a police car was always parked nearby.

As the days passed by everyone began to relax just a little bit and a belief that Spider had either scarpered abroad or hidden somewhere and died from his considerable injuries began to take hold. As a result the police protection was reduced to a regular drive by the pub. The locals stopped talking about what had happened and returned to the usual conversation topics of football and women with the exception of Jock who persisted in offering to move in till Spider's whereabouts were known. Janine slowly relaxed and started to return to her old routine. She had asked one of the regulars to take the rubbish and the empties out of the back door for a while but soon felt safe enough to resume doing this herself. As a result, at the start of one shift, she had left the back door wedged open between trips with rubbish bags, to find that Spider had let himself in.

Janine froze when she saw him. It was before the pub had opened, and the front door was still locked. She looked around for any weapon but saw none. Before she could move, Spider had rushed over and grabbed her by the throat.

"Remember me?" he snarled in her face.

Janine said nothing.

"I asked you if you remembered me," shouted Spider as he tightened his grip on her till she started to choke.

"Yes, I remember you," she managed to whisper.

"We're going to take a little trip, you and I, and we're not going to invite your friends from the cops."

Spider produced a knife from inside his coat.

"If you try to escape I will slit your throat and leave you bleeding where you fall. Is that clear?"

Janine was terrified but managed to nod.

Spider moved his hand from her throat to her upper arm, grabbing it so tight that she gasped in pain.

"Let's go, sweetheart," said Spider in such a calm manner that it was more terrifying than if he had shouted it in her face.

Janine wracked her brains for some way to break free or raise the alarm but Spider had her in a viciously tight grip and was clearly too strong for her to wrestle with.

He pushed her firmly in front of himself towards the back door, opening it slightly to look out. All he could see were parked cars. He pushed the knife into

Janine's side till it broke the skin and drew blood. She could feel a trickle of blood run down the inside of her promotional Guinness tee-shirt. It wasn't life threatening but clearly, struggling with Spider would be.

"No nonsense or I'll push it all the way in. Understand?"

Again Janine managed somehow to nod despite being terrified.

Spider pushed her through the back door and guided her painfully towards a parked blue Mondeo nearby, unaware that they were being watched every step of the way.

Chapter Thirty Three

George kept the new car immaculate inside and out as he tried to work up the courage to ask Janine out. The three girls had decided to move out of George's home and into Evelyn's flat. Apparently it had always been in her name and it seemed to make sense all round for them all to use it, with Rosie and Carol paying rent and generally keeping an eye on her. As a result George's flat resorted to its old bachelor pad status. He missed the female touch about the place, and he managed to keep up some of the recent improvements regarding cleanliness and fresh smells throughout, but it was not the same. Part of him wanted to think that Janine might consider moving in on whatever basis she wanted. The other, more experienced part of him still regarded it as impossible that any women would regard him as a catch of any kind.

This inner conflict continued in the same way for several weeks after the car had been bought and although he continued to go to The Ranch for his darts games he found the visits uncomfortable occasions of failed opportunity.

Eventually he was watching breakfast news when an American lifestyle coach was interviewed about his latest book. George was ready for some gobshite shouting at everyone to get off their backside and do something with their lives, probably in time to suitable music. He was surprised however, to find the guru was a fairly soft spoken individual whose personal life story was not the stuff of Jeremy Kyle but instead was one of comfortable middle class normality. He was inspired to help others, apparently, by his own fortune in work, finance and family life. A student of psychology, he had been struck by the number of people, male and female, who lived alone in the overpopulated cities and towns. His book was a handbook of how to find someone in the crowd and how to get the courage together to talk to them and maybe find a life partner. George took in every word and five minutes after the interview had finished he had ordered a copy of the book online for next day delivery.

It seemed to be a long 24 hours or so till the book arrived but when it did George tore off the wrapper and read it from cover to cover in a day taking notes as he went. He crashed into his bed that night with very tired eyes but with a resolve to ask Janine out whatever the outcome.

The next day he cleaned the car yet again and showered and dressed himself twice before heading for The Ranch at a time in the late morning when Janine was likely to be on her own, or at least when the place might be very quiet. He had a number of opening comments and topics written down with which to start a conversation and had thought through all the replies that he could get in return. He felt confident and motivated in a way he never had before. Today was the day. It was now or never and if Janine turned him down he was ready and could cope. After all there were plenty more fish in the sea.

He checked off the list of ideas from reading the book and took one last look in the mirror before heading out to the sparkling car and driving cautiously to towards The Ranch. He had a steely look in his eye and knew he was ready for this. As he approached the pub he headed towards the quiet street to the rear where people tended to park. He stopped the car near the back door of the pub and looked through his list again just to make sure he was 100% ready. Despite his new found confidence he was still a little bit nervous and he felt his mouth was slightly dry as a result. He reached over to a bag he had brought with him and took a sip of water from a large plastic bottle. Then he sprayed his mouth with just a hint of breath freshener. He checked his flies. He checked his tie. He checked the large bouquet of flowers ("Take a large bouquet of flowers when you ask her out on a first date. All women love flowers and it removes all doubt about whether or not this is a romantic occasion"). Then he read through his list one more time. Although he was nervous he knew that this time his new American friend had given him the confidence to actually go through with it. He was ready to ask Janine out and nothing was going to stop him. Nothing.

As he took his seatbelt off and reached for the door handle he was surprised to see Janine leave the pub through the back door with another man holding her arm.

"Bugger," he thought. "Too late!"

Then he looked closer at the man, who had a strange look about him. He had lost his hair at the back and right hand side and had some large plasters on the other side. Then he froze. It was the tattooed man George had hit with the credit card reader and Janine had knocked out with the coffee jug.

"Shit," thought George to himself, realising that it was unlikely Janine was heading out on a date.

As the unlikely couple reached a blue Mondeo parked near the rear door of The Ranch, the man opened the driver's door and roughly forced Janine inside before getting into the seat directly behind her. As he did so George noticed the glint of a knife in Spider's hand. Once inside Janine was handed the car keys and obviously instructed to drive. The car slowly pulled out of its parking space and headed right at the end of the side street towards the junction of the main road.

George followed on, out of sight and desperately wondering what to do. Phone the police he thought. They'll know what to do. He reached into his pocket for his mobile phone before remembering one of the things on his check list.

"Don't use your mobile phone on a first date. It is very rude and shows a lack of respect for your date. In fact leave it behind to make sure your full attention is directed towards the lady opposite you."

"American bastard !" hissed George under his breath, thinking of his phone sitting uselessly on his sideboard. "Now what do I do?"

For the moment he followed the blue car in front, making sure he didn't lose it at any of the lights. This involved driving far faster than he was used to doing and took most of his concentration. It also involved driving through a couple of red lights. George was terrified. What if he lost the car? What if Spider realised he was being followed and attacked Janine at a set of lights? What if none of that happened and George had to confront him again? There were no good options here but he had to keep up with the blue car whatever it took. Yet again he had been put in a position where he was Janine's only hope.

George judged that Spider must have ordered Janine to drive carefully as he found he was able to keep up with them reasonably easily. They drove through

Coatshill and out onto the M74 heading towards Glasgow. George was able to drop back a bit behind another car while still keeping sight of the Mondeo up ahead. He was still terrified of what would happen. He had no clear plan.

The blue car continued on the M74 towards the south side of Glasgow while most of the traffic took the off ramp and swung round towards the M8 and the North side. George found himself without another car to hide him but hoped he was staying far enough behind to avoid suspicion. He saw the car take the off ramp for Cambuslang and head down the slope towards the roundabout.

"Where was he taking her?" he wondered as he followed behind.

Ahead of him he could see the blue Mondeo slowing down behind a queue of other cars in front, each waiting for their turn to go round the roundabout. It looked like Spider was heading for the East End of Glasgow.

In front of the blue car was a small, white Fiat Cinquecento and ahead of that was a police BMW patrol car with a white transit van in front of it at the edge of the roundabout. George saw the police car and wondered if he could swerve round to the left and speed ahead and catch the police officers' attention. He had to rule out that course of action because he couldn't get past on the left hand lane due of the speed and volume of traffic there. He was rapidly approaching the back of the queue of traffic and was running out of time. Stopping and trying to run round to the police car was a non-starter too as it might pull away by the time he dragged his old bones down there. That would also give the game away to Spider that he had been followed. As time for decision making started to run out George had a sudden brainwave.

. . . .

Miss Blackery had been living on her nerves for some time now, what with all the comings and goings at the flat next door. It had been bad enough with the dodgy people visiting that nasty Mr Cook and his poor sister. Mr Wilson on the ground floor was no help as he was virtually housebound and the nice new couple, The Caldwells had only lasted a few weeks. After the horrific events of her neighbour's murder she was quite beside herself with worry. The police had been very reassuring and had had an officer outside the flats for a while afterwards. A nice woman officer had visited to take Miss Blackery's statement and had also called a few times after that to reassure her that she was safe in her own home.

It had helped for a while but eventually Miss Blackery had started to think she should move from her flat. It took her some time to come round to this way of thinking, as she had been happy there for a long time before Mr Cook had moved in and did not want to be chased away. However, it had come to the point where she raised the subject of moving with her widowed sister who lived close to Cambuslang. They had talked on the phone about how neither of them was getting any younger. Maybe they should consider sharing a house, perhaps the larger one in Cambuslang or a new one near the seaside with ground floor access. They would be company for each other and as one of them would inevitably need more care in the years ahead it would be comforting to know that a sister was on hand to provide it and deal with local services. Miss Blackery would not be able to drive her little white Cinquecento forever and living with her sister on a ground floor would make giving it up far easier. On balance it was an idea that they should meet up and discuss and so it was decided that Miss Blackery would visit her sister and stay over for a few days to talk things through. It would also provide an opportunity to see if they could cope with the invasion of even a sister into their previously independent existences. With enough clothes packed in her little car and some homemade jams as gifts for her sister, Miss Blackery had headed off that day leaving 10 Woodend Walk with a certain sense of relief. Her car was fairly new and immaculately maintained. It did not have one single dent or scratch on it; a fact that Miss Blackery was immensely proud of as a driver now well into her 70s. She called it Tinkerbelle as it could transport her anywhere she wanted to go. She liked her car. She loved it really as if it were a pet cat.

....

George took his foot off the brake and switched it to the accelerator when he was about 30 feet behind the Mondeo. He braced himself and hoped that Janine would somehow be able to do the same. He heard and felt the impact as his car hit the blue car in front and then he lost sight of what was happening ahead as his airbag inflated with a bang. He found that time had somehow slowed down and he could feel the crunch as his car collided with the blue Mondeo in front. In the slow motion world of a car crash he found he was aware of all that was going on and was able to keep his foot on the accelerator to continue the forward motion.

In the blue Mondeo both Spider and Janine were taken completely by surprise as the car behind them failed to stop in time and rear-ended them at speed. Both of them were thrown first backwards then forwards by the impact Janine eventually impacting with the hot balloon of an airbag and Spider into the head restraint of the driver's seat. In their own slow motion world they were aware that the car was still moving.

The now joined together Mondeo and Focus ploughed forward and hit Tinkerbelle with a solid impact which caught Miss Blakery completely by surprise. She had been lost in her thoughts of a future living with her sister. She had never been in any form of road traffic accident before and it was an unpleasant surprise to experience it now at the age of 74. Her head was thrown backwards then forwards into a hot airbag, dislodging her hearing aids and making her wet her pants in shock.

PC Colin Watson and his colleague in the passenger side PC Jim "Big Jim" Cleland had 28 years of policing experience between them, 16 as traffic cops. They had driven deliberately at 30 in built-up areas to slow down the rest of the traffic. They had screamed through built-up areas in hot pursuit of villains and joy riders at speeds of over 70 miles an hour. On motorways they had torn after speeding cars at anything up to 140 miles an hour. Neither had ever been in a crash of any kind although they had often caught up with their prey after they had misjudged a corner or junction. They were both proud of their driving records. All their professional driving had been done in new performance cars maintained in peak condition, ready for them to sound the siren, switch on the blue flashing lights and floor the accelerator. They had driven many nice cars over the years but both agreed that the BMW X5 which had been entrusted to their care was the most impressive to date. They took it turns to drive it, jealous of the other partner's time at the wheel. They were both trained and qualified as Police Drivers and instructors and took their job very seriously indeed. It was therefore something of a surprise for both of them when they were tailgated at a roundabout by the three cars behind them.

Surprised and somewhat annoyed too, as the airbags inflated in their pride and joy, ripping the beautifully laid-out dashboard apart as they inflated. After a moment or two, unhurt but raging, they stepped outside the vehicle, putting their hats on as they went to see who was to blame for what had happened.

A lot of things had happened outside the police car while Colin and Jim had waited for the shock and explosive gasses to disperse from inside the BMW. George had recovered his composure first and had leapt out of his car as quickly as he could. Almost as quickly Janine had seen her best chance of escape and managed to get out of the Mondeo where she tripped and fell onto the verge. Spider, showing the unhuman strength which only top athletes and psychopaths possess had managed to regain focus and was heading after Janine through the rear door of the car when George tripped him up. Miss Blackery, in complete defiance of her advancing years had recovered her thoughts sufficiently to release her seat belt, grab her umbrella and slowly exit the Cinquecento in order to confront the slayer of Tinkerbelle.

Spider looked round at George as he fell and had a sudden recovery of memory.

"You, ya bastard," he shouted and jumped to his feet.

George realised that not only had Spider forgotten for a second about Janine but that he had also instead focused on killing him. With thoughts of the tyre wrench in his own car George headed back up the line of ruined cars to try to get it, with Spider in hot pursuit. Janine, with some incredulity, recognised George and got up and ran after them both. Just before George made it to the car with little chance of retrieving and using the tyre wrench as a weapon, Janine managed to trip Spider again. As he fell he looked round again, and like a dog that can only chase one stick at a time he rose to his feet to try and grab Janine. This gave George just enough time to grab the first potential weapon he could find, the water bottle, and bring it down on Spider's head with as much force as he could muster. This time as Spider fell he looked round to see a little old lady advancing on the three of them with an old fashioned umbrella. Janine started hitting Spider with her fists before he hit the grass verge.

As Miss Blackery reached the three struggling figures beside the rearmost vehicle of the pile-up she tried to assess what she saw. There was the nice young man who had said hello to her outside her flat one day. He and a fairly respectable looking lady were attacking an evil looking thug on the ground whom she also recognised as a regular visitor to her late and not very lamented neighbour Mr Cook.

With a keen instinct and a thirst for revenge over the damage to Tinkerbelle she looked at George and asked, "Is this the villain who caused the accident?"

Almost entirely deaf without her hearing aids and having already made up her mind she paid no attention to George's reply. Instead she started hitting Spider with her umbrella and when that didn't seem to hurt him enough kicked him a few times with her winter boots.

Jim and Colin climbed out of the still smoking BMW intent on retribution. What they saw took even them by surprise. They had both seen and had to deal with road rage on numerous occasions over the years but this was out with even their scope of experience. They saw a mean-looking thug, with hair on only one side of his head, on the ground trying to get up but being attacked by a well-dressed, middle aged man in a suit wielding an empty plastic water bottle and a rather attractive lady of about the same age in a tight black skirt and Guinness tee-shirt. Between them was a little old lady who could have been Tweetie Pie's owner alternating between kicking the man on the ground and hitting him with her umbrella. They looked at each other.

"Better call for back-up," said Big Jim.

As usual when back-up was needed, Colin radioed the situation in as quickly as possible before returning to assist his colleague. Big Jim would walk slowly forward looking as large and imposing as possible and hope that his approaching figure would intimidate any warring factions sufficiently to calm them down. It was a plan that worked nine times out of ten. Today, however, was one of the rogue tens. He walked forward assessing the situation and assuming the man on the ground was the cause of the crash. The other two obviously knew each other and must have been travelling in the blue car which was hit first. Tweety Pie's owner must be in some kind of shock after being hit whilst driving the small Fiat. In the circumstances there was only one thing to do. Let everyone really hurt the son of a bitch who had trashed the BMW before stopping it and hauling everyone to the police station except the little old lady, who would obviously need medical attention for shock at the nearest hospital.

Jim slowed his pace a little bit to allow everyone from the crash to vent their feelings. As he did so he saw the man on the ground produce a knife from inside his jacket, and swung into action. He brushed Janine aside and grabbed Spider by the arm which held the knife. Spider was taken completely by surprise. So much so that he spun round and punched Big Jim in the face before realising he had been grabbed by a very large policeman.

Big Jim Cleland had only rarely been assaulted in or out of uniform. The result had always been pretty similar for those responsible. Spider found himself feeling the full weight of the law on his face and then his back as he was subdued and very roughly handcuffed. As he lay there in pain with PC Cleland kneeling heavily on the base of his spine, Miss Blackery let fly with one more kick before Janine led her away in tears.

Colin Watson reappeared, having organised back-up, an ambulance and recovery for the damaged vehicles, including his beloved new BMW X5. He noted that Jim had cuffed the person responsible for the crash who must have foolishly tried to resist, judging from the black eye and the blood streaming from his nose. The man in the suit was sitting on the bonnet of the rear vehicle, inexplicably holding a large bouquet of flowers while the lady in the tight black skirt and Guinness tee-shirt was comforting the distraught old lady from the Fiat. Apart from the villain squashed under Big Jim, everyone looked to be healthy enough and all the violence had stopped. "Time to take some statements," he thought. "I bet I could pretty much write this one up without even asking." He was about to find out how wrong he could be.

Colin was pleased to notice that the attractive lady with the well-filled tee-shirt was keen to give her version of events first. He took out his electronic notebook, indicated for her to slow down and then started to take down Janine's story from the point at which she arrived at work that morning. As her story unfolded Colin realised this was no ordinary tail-gating.

Realising the nature of Jim's captive he shouted over, "Don't give him a chance Jim, that one's a dangerous bastard."

"No shit," replied Jim, gently rubbing his blackening eye.

"No seriously. His name is Spider Webb and Coatshill are looking for him on a possible murder charge. Looks like kidnapping too by the sound of it."

"Oh, okay," Jim shouted back before whispering in Spider's scorched ear. "Just give me one excuse son, just one and the ambulance will be for you."

In the end, the ambulance was for Spider as his identity was confirmed, his medical status checked and Jimmy Bell's interest duly noted. Apart from all that, Spider collapsed unconscious when Jim Cleland tried to stand him up and walk him to the first police van to arrive.

George and Janine were interviewed separately after the truth emerged and did not have a chance to speak. Janine managed to mouth "thank you" to him before they were driven separately to Coatshill police station to give statements. Miss Blackery took some time to calm down. Eventually though, her sister was summoned and managed to focus her on helping the police to sort out who was to blame for wrecking poor Tinkerbelle. After a brief visit home to shower and change, she too arrived at Coatshill police station to give her statement, crestfallen to have discovered that the accident had been caused by the nice young man in the suit but comforted by the fact that the thug on the ground had been "a wrong un" after all. Somehow, the whole thing was his fault all along.

Chapter Thirty Four

Janine's farewell do at The Ranch was a busy affair. With only a week to go till Christmas there was a genuine panic amongst the regulars that the new owners, a brewery, might not have a team of staff in place to keep their local open over the festive season. Many were genuinely sorry to see Janine leave, viewing it as the end of a golden era. A few were sorry that they might not see her daughter Rosie behind the bar ever again in her mini skirt, jeggings or skin-tight jeans. For a few of the less well recognised faces it was clearly the attraction of bar prices matching those of Janine's first night there which had brought them in the door. Whatever had brought them there in the first place it was clear that The Ranch was having its busiest night for a long time and that those who were there were there for a good time.

Janine was rightly the centre of attention and was being gracious with all the wishes of good luck from her regulars and dealing well with the hugs and squeezed bottoms that she was experiencing too with equal good grace. She was also managing to introduce Steve the new manager and his wife Maureen who were making a point of meeting everyone they could while Janine was still there and stayed sober throughout the whole event.

Nobody seemed to be concerned by the recent demise of one of the regulars, one Frankie Cook and his occasional drinking companion Willie McBride. Certainly no one made mention of it to Steve and Maureen. No, tonight was about having a good time and wishing a suitable farewell to The Ranch's greatest ever landlady, Janine McGovern. Cheap drinks and free food were a secondary consideration, as was the presence of Janine's daughter Rosie who seemed destined to continue working there, accompanied by her equally attractive friend Carol. All was well and nobody wanted to spoil the atmosphere.

There was, however, a brief moment of concern when Jimmy Bell walked into the bar, but he was dressed in a very casual open neck shirt and was carrying a bouquet of flowers and a card which quickly established that he was off duty and was here simply to wish Janine all the best. He smiled and held up the flowers and card so that all the locals could see, and they visibly relaxed. Willie Taylor walked over and insisted on buying him a drink.

In a quiet moment he handed the bouquet and the card to Janine and gave her a brief kiss on the cheek before sitting down next to her and George in one of the side booths.

"You can relax now," he said. "Spider is going to court for murder, kidnapping and a string of assaults. A whole load of people have come forward as witnesses now that Frankie and Willie are out of the way. He'll never get out even if he survives inside. I gather there are a number of people in Barlinnie and elsewhere with scores to settle with him. The Glasgow Police have a good crowd of folk in jail and are happy too. Unfortunately the main player, Simmons, got away somehow but he knew nothing about you two. He'll reappear again sometime like the proverbial bad penny and they'll be waiting for him. Anyway, I'll leave you two together; apparently I'm next on the darts. Good luck to you both and thanks."

With that Jimmy smiled, stood up and left them alone together, winking at George as he went. He headed for the dart board and tried not to groan out loud when he realised he was paired with Old Jock.

"What will you do now?" asked George once Jimmy had left them alone.

"Not sure really," she replied in all honesty. "With the pub being sold to a chain I have to move out of the flat tomorrow and find somewhere else to live. I've organised a couple of nights in a local B&B to give me time to think, then I'll have to make a decision. Pretty much anything but the pub trade, really."

Janine smiled a genuine smile and added, "But don't worry about me, I'm a survivor. I never really had a chance to thank you for all your help that day when Spider showed up, and with Rosie and that Frankie Cook. It's ironic that she and Carol are going to move in with his sister Evelyn, but it seems like a win:win situation. Thank you."

Janine stood up and kissed George on the cheek.

"It was a pleasure having a house full of people for a change," said George. "I'll miss the company to be honest about it."

After a pause he added, "Of course now I have a spare room if you're stuck. I'm just saying I wouldn't want you to rush into anything which meant you had to move away or that."

George went a slightly reddish colour.

"I've taken advantage of your kindness enough, George Milne," said Janine. "I don't want to put you out any more."

As she said it Janine looked deeply into George's eyes in a way that few women had ever done before.

"You wouldn't be putting me out," he assured her. "Not at all."

"I'm allergic to cats," said Janine with an apologetic look on her face, "and I know how fond you are of them."

"Not a big problem," said George with a smile. "I can live without them. Honestly I can."

"You are such a nice guy George," Janine added. "But if I moved into your spare room would I be safe?"

George stared back into her eyes and said, "Only as safe as you wanted to be."

"That's good enough for me," said Janine, squeezing his knee in a deliciously sexy way. "And don't worry about money; I've managed to spirit away enough to keep us comfortable for a while."

"I've got a bit put by myself," countered George.

"A bit tucked under the mattress eh?" said Janine.

George nodded, "Pretty much spot-on."

"Well, whatever happens and whatever we do, I insist on paying my share, 50:50," said Janine. "I want to be equal partners in our future."

She raised her glass and toasted, "To our future, George Milne. Let's be happy for the rest of our lives."

George liked everything she had said so far that night, especially the 50:50 arrangement and the way she squeezed his knees. "To our future, Janine McGovern. To happiness."

At that moment Willie Taylor appeared with his wife Alison and gauging the mood of the occasion correctly as usual, hugged them both separately and accused of George of being a sly dog, which he rather liked the sound of. Alison hugged them both too although she hardly knew them and wished them, "Every happiness".

The night went on and on in good spirits throughout and at the end of it George found himself being led up the stairs to the staff flat for the kind of evening he had only previously associated with New Year but with none of the resultant fall out.

The next day he went home to prepare his house for the arrival of the most welcome guest he could imagine, after a night that surpassed his wildest expectations of good nights.

A mad morning of cleaning was followed by a quick smash and grab shopping expedition and some final preparations of both himself and the flat. At 5 o'clock, after a smooth hand over to Steve and Maureen, Janine arrived with all her worldly goods piled into a taxi. For no apparent reason George insisted on carrying her over the threshold and they consummated her arrival on the sofa before collecting her luggage from the front garden and paying a slightly embarrassed taxi driver.

Once the door closed behind them they sat side by side on the sofa laughing.

"Is this happiness?" asked George.

"I hope so," replied Janine. "Because if it is it depends on nobody else but us," and she kissed George full on the lips the way he was starting to enjoy.

"So, should I put my stuff in your spare room?" she asked with a wicked look in her eyes.

"Probably," replied George, "That'll give us more room to make love in mine."

They laughed and kissed some more.

"Oh, I bought you a present," said George. "I wasn't sure what to get you so it's a bit of a wild shot."

He handed Janine a carefully wrapped parcel with a bow on top.

"For me?" she asked with genuine emotion. "I haven't had a present from a man in ages."

She carefully unwrapped it and, irritatingly for George, folded the wrapping paper before finally revealing the present inside. It was a zebra patterned onesie, size medium.

She smiled at him with a warmth that he had not previously known.

"I always wondered what it would feel like sleeping in one of those," she said and disappeared to the bathroom to try it on.

When she returned she was wearing it with the front slightly open.

"It's so warm," she said. "I don't think I'll ever wear anything else in bed from now on."

"I was hoping you might say that," said George and led her to his bedroom.

Chapter Thirty Five

Evelyn awoke on Christmas morning after one of the best and most peaceful night's sleeps she had ever had. Looking at the clock she saw that it was already after ten o'clock. Through force of habit she waited in her bed to listen for the sound of arguing or fighting coming from the next rooms. After a good few minutes she heard nothing and also realised that she didn't have to worry about that any more. She slowly got up and put on her fluffy slippers, then went through to the front room.

Rosie and Carol had got up much earlier and exchanged gifts. With shrieks and giggles they had each unwrapped a new animal pattern onesie. Then still giggling and with much tickling and playful spanking they had stripped off the matching zebra onesies and put on their new Christmas presents there and then. Thus it was that when Evelyn entered the living room she found Rosie dressed as a Giraffe and Carol dressed as a monkey trying to do an impression of one scratching and swinging through the trees.

The two friends looked round at Evelyn and laughed out loud. Then they rushed over and gave her a big hug.

"Merry Christmas, Evie - come and open your presents," invited Rosie still with her hand protectively round Evelyn's shoulders.

Evelyn looked round the front room in disbelief. Her flatmates had erected and decorated a huge real Christmas tree during the night while she slept. From each corner of the room to the next hung paper-chains and Chinese style lanterns dangled from each corner. There were candles on the mantelpiece and tinsel hanging from every ornament and picture. Evelyn gasped in amazement and gave each of the other girls a massive hug in turn.

She had always dreaded Christmas as a child. It was a full day she had to spend in the same house as her father who would be drunk from mid-morning. On the rare occasions that her mother put up decorations, they were cheap and sparse at best and always the target for her father's temper as the day wore on. It was almost a ritual that he would tear them down in a rage at some point in the day and beat up Evelyn and her mother or worse.

After her father had disappeared on that trip with Frankie and Willie, her mother had rarely made an effort. By then she was permanently drunk or in hospital being treated for alcoholism or an associated accident. Frankie had tried each year to make Christmas a special day for Evelyn but his busy work schedule meant he was often away or in hiding over the festive season.

As a result she looked at her front room and knew that this was the best Christmas morning she had ever known. The girls led her over to the big chair beside the fire where she liked to sit and watch television and sat her down. There were plenty of parcels under the tree and Raven was happily playing with the curly ribbon on one of them, while all the time keeping an eye on something out of Evelyn's sight behind the couch.

Once Evelyn was sitting comfortably the girls began. They brought out one present at a time and passed it to whoever's name was writing on the label. There were presents for all of them from each other, from George and Janine and from some of the regulars at The Ranch. There was even a present for Raven from someone called Jimmy Bell, addressed in brackets "to Santa's little helper".

The girls opened the presents amid shrieks and giggles and gasps. George seemed to have spent a lot of money on jewellery and perfumes for them all and, no doubt with Janine's help, had made a series of inspired choices. Janine had shown the steady eye of a mother's taste with the clothes she had bought them. They laughed and giggled and showed off the presents they had received to each other as they went.

When all the parcels from under the Christmas tree had been handed out and opened, Carol looked round at Rosie.

"Is it time do you think?" she asked.

"I think so," replied Rosie.

The two girls stood up and moved till they could reach round the couch. From its hiding place there they retrieved a carrying cage with a tiny puppy sound asleep inside.

"We thought you might like some company while we are out at work," said Rosie.

"It's a boy and he doesn't have a name yet, so you'll need to think of one, although there is no rush."

Evelyn stood up and walked over to the carrier and gently reached inside. She delicately picked up the puppy, managing not to wake it as she did so and sat down again on her chair. Raven came over and jumped up on her lap, sniffing cautiously at the new arrival. Evelyn stroked them both equally so neither would get jealous. Rosie and Carol each sat on one of the arms of the chair and gave her a hug.

"You'll be safe now," said Rosie. "Nobody's ever going to hurt you again," and she kissed Evelyn gently on the top of her head.

Evelyn looked round still smiling uncontrollably. She looked at her friend the giraffe and her friend the monkey. Then she looked at her cat Raven and her new puppy and at her own reflection seeing a zebra smile back. Then she looked up, because someone had once told her that was where all dead people went.

"You did it Frankie," she whispered. "You kept your promise."

The End

<u>George Milne – Murder at the Butler's Convention</u>

Just when George believes he can safely return to his mundane existence, adventure strikes again. The exotic Lola Cortez aka Theresa Maguire enters his life and not only threatens his peace and quiet in front of the television but also his new found relationship with Janine. Add to this a serious of seemingly unconnected murders where George is the prime suspect and he is soon fighting for his freedom. Can he make it safely back to his cup of tea and biscuits?

Lola Cortez had been born and christened Theresa Maguire in the Drumchapel district of Glasgow. Her mother had given birth almost exactly nine months after a holiday in the Spanish resort of Lloret de Mar. Theresa never knew her father and suspected in later life that her mother may not have been too certain either as to who he was. What she did grow up knowing was that her mother loved Spain, loved the Spanish people and language and loved Spanish men in particular.

<u>The Treasure Hunters</u>

A small and apparently sleepy village becomes the focus in the search for missing CIA funds. Someone local has 'got rich quick' but the security services can't broadcast their loss without admitting what is going on nearby and have to try to discover who without raising any suspicions. Robbie Buchanan is blackmailed out of medical retirement to track down the cash, but has his training in MI6 prepared him for everything the village of Kirkton has in store?

Roddy Murray's third book takes a riotous route through village life as cultures clash and the big, wide world meets its match.

The permutations of who was living or sleeping with whom and who had previously been living or sleeping with who else seemed endless according to some people's accounts. Robbie was glad, however, for the piece of advice Jennifer had given him about arriving in a small village: "Always assume you are talking to someone related to whoever you are talking about and you won't go far wrong."

<u>Body and Soul</u>

Two very different men are on a pathway to a meeting which will change both their lives forever. One is a Scottish ex-soldier, ex-boxer, ex-husband, ex-father and ex-drunk struggling to turn his life around. The other, the CEO of an American multi-national, has both wealth and power. They do not know each other and only the American believes he knows the true purpose of their meeting. In fact both have been duped in different ways and as their lives begin to unravel they must try to deal with the truth if they can. Only one has the skills and determination to survive.

After failing to wake Frank he dragged him into the shower which conveniently only produced cold water and turned it on full. The effect wasn't immediate, but slowly the old fighting, kicking Frank began to re-appear, curse the first house guest he had had for six months and try to throw him out. After an initial but futile attempt to punch Paddy's lights out Frank calmed down enough to recognise his visitor.